DOG LOT

DOG LOT

A NOVEL

DENNIS GIMMEL

COURT STREET PRESS
MONTGOMERY

Court Street Press
P.O. Box 1588
Montgomery, AL 36102

ISBN 1-58838-066-1

Design by Randall Williams
Printed in the United States of America

TO MY SWEET WIFE,

ROSEMARY

WITHOUT HER LOVE, SUPPORT, EDITING SKILLS, AND BELIEF

IN WHAT I WAS DOING, THIS WORK COULD NOT HAVE BEEN DONE.

SPECIAL THANKS TO THESE FRIENDS

WHO HELPED MAKE THIS A BETTER BOOK:

ANGIE WOOD, MARY SMITH, CARA LENFESTY,
KEN AND KAY BROWN, KAYE JOHNSON, DONNA
HUMES, AND SHANNON HAIRR

CHAPTER I

Jake Brown hadn't had a bite all day. But he didn't care. His friends said, "Jake, you're gonna hate retirement. Doing nothing is gonna get old real fast." That was three years ago and it hadn't gotten old yet. Jake never shied away from work but he wasn't afraid of play either. His dad was like that. It was a good trait to pass on.

On the Third Avenue Pier Jake was known as one of the "pier rats." He had been called a lot worse. The hard core "pier rats" were on the pier all day everyday, but not Jake. He showed up maybe three days a week and he might spend two or three hours out there, just long enough to say "hello" to a few of his derelict pals. He had always been attracted to strange people.

Speaking of strange, take old Joe for example. Joe Lane, a fellow pier rat and local terror, just pulled up the biggest wad of fishing lines and old rusty hooks and barnacles that anyone had ever seen. Not only that, but the "Einstein" was staring at it two inches from his face and saying something about somebody's mother.

Jake had known some anti-social characters in his day, but Joe Lane took the cake. Half the time when Jake spoke to him he wouldn't answer and when he did answer Jake wished he hadn't.

"What you got there, Joe?" Jake asked not really expecting an answer.

"You truly are stupid, aren't you?" grunted Joe.

"Thank you, and I like you, too," Jake responded.

"It so happens I got a monstrosity here, or for an ignoramus like you, I got a mess," Joe barked.

Joe thrived on stuff like this. He was just about that sick. No doubt he was figuring how many salvageable parts were in it. It looked like it had been down there for years. It probably hadn't though. The salt water could certainly rust things in a hurry.

"At least you caught something. I'm sure that's more than anyone else on the pier can say," Jake ventured.

"Old Lady Hubbard caught a little shark," Joe said. "She's so damn ugly though the thing jumped back in as soon as it got a good look at her. That is the ugliest woman I have ever seen and I've seen some ugly women in my day."

Jake could definitely believe that. When it came to ugly, Joe was like a magnet. The exception was his wife Jane who was a genuinely nice woman, good looking too for a woman pushing sixty. Joe griped about her everyday but even he had enough sense to know what he had.

She got sick last year and had to have a breast removed. Jake went up to see her and Joe at the hospital. Thankfully she seemed to get through it okay.

"How's the private eye business?" Joe smiled.

He knew darn well that Jake hadn't had any work in seven months. And even then it was about as close to nothing as you could get. Some gal from North Myrtle wanted to find a cousin she hadn't seen or heard from in twenty-five years. Jake checked a few things on the Internet, made a phone call, made the connection, and collected his check. It took all of five hours.

"It's been kind of slow, Joe. I'm sure you can relate to slow." Jake was a bit of a smart mouth himself.

The truth of the matter was that business had been terrible. What the heck, Jake was retired. He saw an advertisement on TV promoting a private eye school. For the umpteenth time he was suckered into something and sent his money in. He went through the course and received a diploma. The real crazy thing was the State of South Carolina must have thought it was the real deal. He sent them forty-five dollars and became a certified private eye. The fools even sent him a certificate.

Jake actually had five job assignments in the twenty-six months since he'd been a private eye. Just nickel-and-dime stuff mostly. Trail my husband, etc. It was not really dangerous. It could be. But they don't pay him enough to be a hero. It did liven up his life somewhat.

Joe looked up from the tangle in front of him with his poop eat'n grin and terrible teeth. "I bet it's hard to find people stupid enough to pay you, even in this God-forsaken place. You might think about paying them. Jane might pay you to tail me."

"She couldn't pay me enough to trail your sorry hind end. Besides, all anyone would have to do to find you is stick their nose into the wind and take a whiff."

"And you love it, don't you?" Joe retorted.

"What time they running us out of here today?" Jake asked, sensing a need to elevate the conversation.

"I think Bimbo's gonna let us stay till dark. Ain't that special?"

"Well, I'm not gonna be able to stick around. I got things to do," Jake said. "Some of us have a life."

As Jake reeled in his line and got his stuff together Joe just laughed. "You're pathetic. No wonder you worked for the Post Office. Nobody else would take you." Joe loved to crack on Jake. "Don't leave yet. I think I see your Christmas present," he said as he stared into the tangled web.

"I love a surprise. See you next time," Jake said heading off of the pier.

Jake's old Toyota truck really did need a bath. The smell was even getting to him. One of those funky air fresheners probably wouldn't hurt. Maybe tomorrow he would clean the thing up. It was supposed to be nice weather. October was always nice in Myrtle Beach. Jake had lived in the Carolinas for almost thirty years and he loved the sunshine. He was from up north, Ohio to be exact. Up there beautiful weather in October was a long way from a given.

It was 4 p.m. Tuesday and probably seventy degrees. The traffic on Highway 17 was moderate. During the week traffic was not too bad. On the weekends this time of year Jake always tried to avoid the main drag.

His trip home was a six-mile drive west on 501. He lived in the Meadows, one of those developments built around a golf course. He liked it there. There was something in the Meadows for every pocketbook. Jake lived in the lower end. But it worked for him. He was a man of simple tastes. After all, it was just Jake and Amos.

Amos was his dog. He was a bit of a bird dog that looked like a beagle but had the brain of a basset. He was seven years old and liked Jake. He was in select company.

Pulling into the development, Jake saw the Clarks walking their dog "Mitsy." It had to be the fattest terrier the world had even seen. The dog was eating better than Jake. It had to be. For some reason the Clarks never liked Jake. At least he didn't think they did. They always looked at him like he had communist ties or something. Sometimes Jake would sit on his porch and drink a beer. That might be it. He was not a lush. He just liked to have a beer every now and then, maybe two on Saturday night. Whatever, they just didn't like him.

Jake heard Amos barking when he turned onto his road. The dog always heard his truck just as soon as he pulled into the development and that was a good 300 yards away. Amos was kept in a fenced in yard in the back when Jake was not at home. But when Jake was home Amos stayed in the house. He was good company.

After checking the mail and walking into the house, Jake noticed a message on the phone recorder. "Probably Sally," he thought. Sally was his budding girlfriend. Thumbing through the mail he hit play. "Hello. Is this Strand Private Eye. . . . This is Liz Alton. I live in Chesterfield. I'm at fourteen Victor Lane. I need to talk to you. Please call me. My number is 842-3123. Thank you."

"OOOH, I'm a working man!" Jake said to himself. "Sounds like this gal's got some cash. Not many dumps out there in Chesterfield. I better give her a call before she calls someone else."

"Hello, Ms. Alton. . . . This is Jake Brown, Strand Private Eye. I'm returning your call. . . . I understand. How about tomorrow morning. . . . about ten. . . . That would be great. . . . No, I know how to get there. Yes, near Litchfield, yes ma'am . . . yes fourteen Victor. . . . yes. . . . see you then. . . . thank you. . . . goodbye."

"She's got to be loaded!" Jake said to Amos. This called for a hotdog and a beer.

~

Wednesday morning brought another beautiful day at the beach. Jake never took the Carolina weather for granted. Probably had something to do with all those years he spent in Ohio.

Amos woke Jake up every morning. The dog would sit by the bed and wait for him to open his eyes and then just stare at him until Jake started to move. The dog had him figured out. He knew he was nuts.

Jake left the house about 9 that morning giving himself just enough time to grab a cup of coffee and hot biscuit at his favorite stop.

The Beach Deli on Highway 17 was busy as usual. It was one of those small places that all the locals love and the tourists don't know about.

In Jake's mind the real attraction at the Beach Deli was not the biscuits. It was Jill. What a doll. She was twenty-eight with long dark hair, a slim figure, a gorgeous smile, and was friendly to everyone. She made him wish he were thirty years younger.

"Hey Jake," Jill said with a sparkle. "What would you like this morning?"

He didn't have the guts to tell her the truth. "A sausage biscuit and coffee. You look great as usual." What an understatement that was.

He picked up a paper that was lying on the counter and noticed that his team was all banged up for their upcoming game. What else was new? His mutual fund was up one quarter.

"Here you go, darling," she said to him.

"She must get off on driving me crazy," Jake thought. "It's probably the easiest thing she does all day." He was certainly not alone. She was a certified heartbreaker. "I think she does like me a little bit," he rightly thought. But he was way too old for her. He'd be sixty in a few months.

"You playing golf today?" Jill asked as she took the stool beside him.

"No, not today. I got a private eye job today down at Chesterfield!"

"You dog you! How'd you manage that? You bribing old women again?"

"I ain't got enough money to bribe that crowd and I don't think I'm quite that good looking."

"I don't know about that," she said as she pecked him on the cheek and got up to go back to work.

"Someone needs to put that woman in prison," he thought to himself as he threw her a wink on his way out.

∼

Chesterfield Estates was a haven for millionaires. It was a gated community of fifty homes, none of them for under a half million. Jake found fourteen Victor Lane without any problem. It was a beautiful new home that looked to be about fifty yards long and it backed up to the sixth tee box. A new Lexus sat in the drive complementing the perfect landscaping.

"Yes," said a sweet black lady who answered the door.

"Yes, I'm Jake Brown. Ms. Alton is expecting me."

"Please come in and have a seat. She will be right with you," she said.

"So this is what cold cash looks like?" Jake thought looking around. He was glad he got to see it before he died. Everything looked so solid, not a speck of dust on anything. It looked like they were expecting somebody from the "Home and Garden Club" to walk in any minute.

"Mr. Brown?" Liz Alton asked as she walked confidently into the room. "Thank you so much for coming."

"My pleasure."

Liz Alton was a striking woman in her mid-fifties. She had perfect short blond hair, brown eyes, slim figure, and nice features.

"You have a beautiful home."

"Thank you," she said. "I've been here several years. I saw your ad in the paper. I have a problem that has been worrying me sick. Some strange things have happened in recent months.

"I went to the police. They listened to what I had to say and they were going to check into it. I guess they did some looking around. I don't know. The officer came back a few days later and said they could not find anything. He told me to keep him posted. I felt like they weren't taking me seriously. So that's why I called you."

"I see. What kind of strange things have been happening?"

Liz Alton wrenched her hands, took a deep breath and said, "A year ago this past March I opened the door to get my paper and laying on my door step was a dead cat. It looked to me like the head had been crushed. Needless to say, I was upset. I thought, 'what in the world' . . . I thought maybe someone had run over the cat in the road and thinking it was mine had dropped it on my doorstep. But if they did, they did not ring my doorbell. I was home all night."

"Could it have been there the previous evening?" Jake asked.

"No it was not there at dusk because I always walk in the neighborhood and I always come in the front door. No it was put there sometime during the night or in the very early morning hours."

"I see. What else has happened?"

She looked at Jake as if she didn't want to answer, as if she could hardly believe it herself. "This past February I again opened the door to get my paper. There in front of my door was a pair of blue panties." She was visibly shaking as she told him the story.

"What did you do when you saw them?"

"I just stood there and stared for a few minutes. I was so embarrassed. I was afraid to touch them. I knew they weren't mine. I thought that maybe they belonged to Linda. She's my maid. She usually comes in about nine. I finally picked them up and took them inside. I certainly didn't want anyone else to see them. I thought that maybe she had dropped them when she left the day before around five."

"Were they hers?"

"No," Liz said. "Linda was very upset about it. She thought I should call the police. I figured it wouldn't do any good, and besides it was just too embarrassing. I spent the whole day racking my brain. How in the world could this happen? What could this possibly mean? Is it some prank of a high school kid? I just didn't know. . . . I'm sorry, Mr. Brown, could I offer you a cup of coffee? I have just been so upset over this."

"That's quite all right and you can call me Jake. Coffee would be great. Cream and sugar please."

"I'll be happy to get it and you can call me Liz," she said getting up.

This was definitely not one of Jake's nickel-and-dime cases. Maybe he should tell her he just couldn't handle this. She would find that out on her own soon enough anyway. He should be fishing or playing golf or something, anything but this.

"Linda made some fresh," Liz said as she placed a silver-plated coffeepot on the table.

Jake decided to come clean. "I am really not much of a private eye. You could certainly do better than me. Maybe you could find someone with more experience. I've only been doing this a couple of years and I haven't had many cases. I just don't want you to expect something that I'm not," he said shifting into his self-destruct mode.

Liz put down her coffee cup and said, "I like you, Jake. I've always flown by the seat of my pants. I have a knack for reading people. You, Jake Brown, are a trustworthy, honest person. And even though you have limited experience I am not going to look for someone else. You, me, and God knows who else, are going to figure this thing out."

"Is there more?" he asked.

"I wish there weren't, but there is," Liz said. "Last June I went out to get the mail. I saw the mail carrier go by about forty-five minutes before. I open my mailbox, and in with the mail was a pair of binoculars. Of course I thought the carrier must have left them for some strange reason. I checked with her the next day. She had not and they were not in the box when she came by."

"Why do you think someone would leave those?" Jake asked.

"I don't know. They were not expensive ones. You've got to realize that by this time I'm getting just a little paranoid. Every few months something strange seems to happen. I guess I thought that someone wanted me to think they were spying on me. I just didn't know what to think," she said. She turned away as tears formed in her eyes.

"I'm sorry about all this. I know it must be unsettling."

"Thank you. It has been upsetting. I've never had to deal with anything like this before. I have always been a strong person, but this . . ." she trailed off.

"We can pick this up tomorrow if you want to."

"I'll be fine."

"Were the binoculars the last incident?"

"No," she said as she rose and walked to the front window and fiddled with the blinds. "There was a knife," she said in a whisper.

"Did you say knife?"

"Yes, a knife. A large knife, like you would use to carve a roast."

"When did this happen?"

"Monday. I found it Monday morning," she said turning from the window. "It was on the deck in the back. I found it about ten in the morning. I called the police. They came out and took the knife and checked it for prints but nothing was found." Rubbing her neck she said, "They probably think I'm crazy. I don't know if I could blame them."

"Do you remember the policeman's name?"

"Sergeant Rogers, Rudy Rogers"

"Rudy Rogers. He's the only guy I know on the force," Jake said.

"He seemed like a nice man," Liz said.

"So Rudy wasn't that concerned about the knife?"

Liz sipped her coffee and said, "He was concerned, it's just what could he do? I wasn't killed, no one attacked me. I believe they think I'm a little unbalanced."

"Rudy is a good man. He won't let it rest. Do you have any theories, Liz?"

"Not really," she said. "I just don't have a clue."

"Anything from your past?"

"Nothing that I know about, Jake. My husband owned a paper mill in Georgetown. It employed about half the people in town for most of this century. We always made an effort to treat people well. I'm sure we made some enemies. People come and go, some get fired, some get hurt. We can't control everything. I'm sure some people are upset with us. No one that I know of, however."

"What's the name of the company?"

"Alton Paper, if you can believe it. Harry's father started the company. Needless to say, we've done well by it."

That seemed rather obvious. "Is there anything else you need to tell me?" Jake asked.

"Not really, I just hope you can help me."

"I hope I can too, Liz. If you need anything call me at home. Oh, it might be a good idea if you get a dog. They can hear things we can't."

"I just might think on that. Do you know of a good place to get one?"

"I just might," he winked. "I'll call you tomorrow."

"Thanks, Jake. Talk to you then."

As Jake headed down the walk he remembered they hadn't even discussed a fee. "I guess she figures she can afford me," he reasoned.

CHAPTER 2

Later that evening Jake's friend, Sally McSwain, was busy slicing cucumbers and tomatoes for salad while he was barbecuing chicken. Amos was hoping like crazy for a piece to fall to the ground.

"So, all you can tell me is she lives in Chesterfield. I wouldn't think they'd let you through the gate with that old truck," Sally said.

"I offered the girl at the gate a little action. She let me right on in," Jake lied.

"You better lay off the beer. I can see that," Sally said.

He just smiled. Sally had been good for him. She was about his age, late fifties, good looking and just plain nice company. At this point they were just friends. That's all either of them wanted for now. Someone to just do things with. It had been five years since Betty died. He felt like a part of himself died with her when she went. He was just not ready to get involved emotionally right now. Sally understood. They were taking things slowly.

"I wonder why she's got you doing this work? It would seem she could get some of the big boys to handle this," Sally said as they sat down to enjoy their feast.

"I don't know. I'm sure the thought crossed her mind when she saw me pull in driving my hunk of junk. She's a very nice person. You would like her. She said she just liked me. Said I seemed like a good person, someone she could trust. Pass the sauce. Thanks."

Sally gave him the evil eye, "She good looking?"

"She is a fox with a capital 'F.' It was all I could do to hold myself back."

"I'm sure she felt the same way," Sally replied. Jake had to hand it to Sally. The girl had a tremendous grasp of the obvious. She could sense the raw sexual forces oozing from every pore of his being. This called for another beer. Sally left about 10 and Amos and Jake called it a day around 11:30.

It was raining Thursday morning when Jake got up. His breakfast consisted of bacon, eggs, and coffee. Most of the time he started the day by reading the Bible for a few minutes and then scanning the newspaper headlines. He was definitely a creature of habit.

This thing with Liz Alton had his mind turning. It was probably not just a figment of her imagination. Someone was definitely harassing this nice woman. She was the richest person Jake had ever had a conversation with, and yet she was not the least bit condescending. The hunk of junk that he drove didn't even embarrass her. When you have her kind of cash you don't sweat the small stuff. He figured he'd better call Rudy and find out what his take was on all this.

"Myrtle Beach Police Department. Bertha speaking. How may I direct your call?" the receptionist answered.

"Bertha, so good to hear your voice. May I speak to Sergeant Rogers please? This is Jake Brown."

"Just a moment," Bertha said wondering who in the world Jake Brown was?

Several moments later Rudy answered, "Jake the snake, and how are you this fine morning?"

"I'm my usual wonderful self," Jake replied. "They haven't made you captain yet?"

"It is hard to believe isn't it?" Rudy said. "Sometimes I just can't figure out what's wrong with these people. Hey, I bet I know why you called. You're just itching to give me some of your money on the golf course. Tell me I'm right, Jake."

"Actually Rudy, I need to talk to you about some private eye matters."

"What did you do, catch some guy with his pants down again, or did some woman want you to trail her cat?" Rudy Rogers replied jokingly. Anyone meeting Rudy for the first time would never guess he was policeman, cabdriver maybe, policeman, never.

"No, actually I got a real job this time."

"That's a change of pace," Rudy said.

"You got time for coffee this morning, Rudy? Maybe the Beach Deli at 10?" Jake asked.

"I think I can work it into my schedule."

"Thanks pal, I'll see you there," Jake said.

"Well Amos, the beat goes on," he said rubbing the dog's flea-infested head. The parking lot at the Beach Deli was one-third full when Jake pulled in about 10. He walked in and slid into a seat by the window. Jill was at the end of the counter hooting and hollering with a small army of construction workers. After a few minutes she brought Jake some coffee and rubbed his bald head as she walked away. The girl definitely ruled in this place. She had every man in the place going crazy. What a gal. A couple minutes later Rudy showed up in his cruiser.

Rudy was about Jake's age. He was thin and smoked all the time but seemed to be in good health. He was probably one of those smokers that would live to be ninety.

"I didn't do it," Jake said to Rudy as he sat down.

"It's been a long darn time since you've done anything you could be arrested for," Rudy replied.

"Hey sergeant, you gonna put the cuffs on me today?" Jill said as she set his coffee down.

"You're getting good at reading my dirty little mind aren't you?" Rudy kidded.

"You good-looking men need a menu?" she said with a wink.

"No, what we need is a phone number," Jake said as Jill headed toward more salivating customers. "When are you going to arrest that woman?"

"Soon I hope," Rudy replied as he stirred his coffee. "So what's up?"

"I got a call Tuesday evening from somebody you know, a Liz Alton." Jake studied Rudy for a response. "She told me that she spoke to you a couple times about some strange things going on with her. She seemed pretty upset."

Rudy stirred his coffee, looked at the sports page and said, "Hey, they got a special at Homewood. We can play for thirty-five dollars after 12. We need to do that."

"When are you off next week."

"Thursday," he said.

"Let's do it then," Jake replied. "What about this Ms. Alton?"

"A very nice lady," Rudy replied. "It seems someone definitely has it in for her. We checked what we could. Nothing came up."

"What did you check?"

"We talked to the neighbors, the people at the gatehouse, the maid. Nothing came up. Unfortunately, until it gets more serious, there is just not much more we can do. We can't set a cop out there and wait for the next pair of panties to show up. Come to think of it, that does sound like pretty good duty. I could ease into retirement on that one."

Jake smiled at Jill as she filled his cup, "What about when the next knife shows up, or worse yet, the next guy carrying the knife?"

"Look, I know it's got her torn up, but there is just not much more that we can do right now. We've got problems in this sweet tourist town that have escalated way beyond idle threats," Rudy said with a sympathetic look.

Rudy sipped his coffee and checked out the paper. "What exactly is she paying you to do, Jake?"

"I really don't know. I told her I didn't have much experience, but she seemed to like me so I guess I'm employed."

"How much is she paying you?"

"I don't know. It never came up. I'm not going to take advantage of her. She is just much too nice for that."

"Yeah, lucky for her she is not a jerk. God knows what you would have charged her if she were. So what are you going to do next, mister nice guy?"

"I don't know. I might go down to Georgetown and get a feel for things. She said her husband's family started and operated a huge paper mill down there."

"Yeah, I've been there. It's something else," Rudy said. "It takes up half the town. That woman might be the richest woman in South Carolina. Who knows, she just might be the next Mrs. Jake Brown."

"Yeah, and Jill here might be the next Mrs. Rudy Rogers," Jake said.

"I could stand that!" Rudy said. "I wonder where the line forms?"

"Right behind me. Let's get out of here before we both go nuts," Jake said as they headed out the door. "I'll be talking to you soon."

"Right, I'll catch you later. Keep me posted, and next Thursday I'm going to get some more of your money at Homewood, right?"

"Whatever you say, Rudy. You're the one with the gun, remember?"

CHAPTER 3

Thursday evening Jake called Liz and told her he wanted to ride in to Georgetown to see if he could find out anything. She gave him the names of a couple of folks to contact.

Friday morning after seeing his sugar at the Beach Deli, he made the fifty-minute drive south to Georgetown.

Rudy was right about one thing. Jake didn't have a problem locating the paper mill. It took up all the land west of Main Street. It was a huge dirty place. He drove through the gate past piles of wood and sawdust and came to a dirty brick building with "Security" written across the front. Once inside he asked for Joe Hage and was told it would be about ten minutes.

"Joe Hage. May I help you?" Jake looked up to see a large man who was close to fifty years old and a muscular 250 pounds.

"Yes," Jake said, "My name is Jake Brown. I believe Liz Alton called?"

"Of course, this way." Jake followed the big man into his office.

The wall opposite the door had a photo of Benjamin and Harold Alton standing together at a building dedication in 1950. Both were strong men standing over six feet tall. A group of serious-looking men surrounded them. It was no doubt a proud day in mill history.

"Two of the finest men I've ever known," Joe said. "The old man was out here everyday until he died at ninety-three. His son Harold was a chip off the old block. A man's man. Everybody respected him. All he ever wanted from anyone was a good day's work. He'd do anything for you. Those were great days."

"When did Harold die?" Jake asked.

"He died in 1992. He was seventy-seven. Had a bad ticker. This place hasn't been the same since. Liz sold the place and moved to Myrtle Beach. She did what she had to do."

"Were there any hard feelings?"

"No. No one could blame her. Everybody loved Liz. She was the closest thing to a queen that this county has ever seen. Harold met her in Saint Louis in 1972. They were married that same year. They were very happy. He was old enough to be her daddy, but if ever two people were in love it was them. There were no hard feelings. Everybody loved Liz."

"I guess she told you about what's going on up there?"

"She sure did. Strange, very strange," Joe said.

"Do you think she would be prone to exaggerate?"

"No way. Liz is as solid as they come. Very stable. Somebody has got a thing for her. If I wasn't so darn busy down here, I'd go up there and personally kick some ass," Joe stated with absolute authority.

"No doubt," Jake thought. He would not want to be on this guy's hit list. "Anybody here that you can think of that might have something against Liz or her husband?"

Joe shrugged his huge shoulders, "We've got 7200 workers here right now. I've been head of security for twenty-one years. In that time we've had three murders at the plant, fifteen away from the plant, twenty-three arrests for embezzlement, eight rapes and twelve convicted of armed robbery. We've got ninety-eight percent great people here, but the few bad apples get all the press. There are hundreds of people around here that have something against everybody. But do I know of anyone with a personal vendetta against Liz or Harold? No, I don't."

Jake thanked Joe Hage for his time and headed out for lunch. He found a picturesque place on the river called the Dock. Sherry, a local cutie, took his order and gave him a nice table on the deck with a great view. After finishing off his gumbo, he had one more stop on his list, a Mrs. Millie Stackpole. She lived at thirty-two Cedar Street. He stopped at a gas station and got a drink and a city map. He saw that Cedar Street was on the south side of town. Jake knew without even going there that it would be in the low-income section. The wind usually blew toward the southwest. And that is not where you want to be in a paper mill town. It was definitely the home of cheap real estate. Who Liz Alton knew on that side of town he couldn't help but wonder.

A few minutes later he was in the midst of the ghetto Georgetown style. Row after row of what looked like mill houses in various stages of disrepair adorned the area. He drove down Cedar Street and stopped in front of Millie Stackpole's house. He walked up to the plain frame house and knocked on the door. "What's you want?" said the menacing voice of a young black man standing in the door with baggy pants on and no shirt.

"Is there a Millie Stackpole here?" Jake nervously asked.

"Who wants to know?" the young man asked. "We ain't payin no mo than what we sent you. If you're here looking for mo' money, you better do yo' self a favor and leave!"

"Who is it, Skoo?" Jake heard a woman ask.

"Some honkie. Don't know what he wants," Skoo said.

"What you want with me? Who sent you here?" she said coming to the door.

"Ms. Liz Alton, ma'am," Jake said noticing her surprise. She stared at him with her intense dark eyes.

"Let's talk on the porch swing. Skoo, you just go on inside," Millie said.

Millie Stackpole was a thin black woman in her mid-forties. Her eyes seemed to say that she had seen much more trouble than she would care to remember. She had dark black eyes that were deep with pain. They took a seat on adjoining rockers as Skoo ducked back inside. They sat in silence for several moments. A cool breeze gently rattled the wind chimes on the porch.

"What did Ms. Lizzy want with me?" Millie finally asked.

Good question. Jake couldn't quite figure that one out either. Liz only told him to look Millie up. "I wish I had a good answer for you, Mrs. Stackpole. There have been some things happening to her lately. Kind of strange things. Almost like someone is trying to scare her. They haven't hurt her yet. It seems like someone might be stalking her or something. She told me to check with you to see if you had any ideas. That's all I know."

Millie pulled out a cigarette and lit it up. She took a long drag and contemplated her next words. "Ms. Lizzy always thought I was the eyes and ears of the blacks round here. I worked in the mill all my life up until I hurts myself on the ramp. Messed somethin' up in my back.

"My man, Skoo's daddy, he was wantin to start a union. He was real active. Had a lot of support, especially among the blacks. Of course ol' man Alton he was against it. Some men came down from Memphis, big shot union people. They talked to Billy and some others. We's getting real close for callin a strike. One day Billy was late comin' home. It was not like him. Not like most of the other men out chasin' women. I was worried."

She lit another cigarette and did not say anything for what seemed like ten minutes. "Some of the boys found Billy the next day. He was dead in the brush by Crow Creek. Somebody beat him up real bad. Police said it was a fight over a woman. I knew that wasn't true. I figure it had somethin to do with the union at Alton Mill."

"So they never found out who did it?" Jake asked.

Millie laughed a smoker's laugh, "This is the south boy, one nigger killin' another don't need no investigation. I know Billy would be alive today if he hadn't got involved with no union."

"How does this tie in with Liz Alton?"

"When this stuff came down all the blacks were ready to tear the mill down. Things were getting real bad. Mr. Alton called in all kinds of so-called experts tryin to calm everybody down. He was even willin to talk to some union folks. There was a lot of violence in town over this. People getting hurt everywhere, both black and white. We even made some national news. Billy was getting more respect dead than he did alive.

"One day Ms. Lizzy she calls me out at the mill. She says she wants to talk to me. Says I won't get in trouble. She takes me off in her Bentley and we drive down to a quiet place on the Waccamaw River. She wanted to hear me out. She hardly talked, she just listened. I tells her how much I love Billy, and how heart broke I am. I tell her that I thought Billy being dead had to do with the mill. I talked about everything I could think of. We must have been there for two hours I'd say. . . . After a while she took me back to the mill. Told me she wanted to talk some more tomorrow. We talked like dat for several days. I talked about the trouble an what I heard. Dis rich white woman gave me respect. . . . Anyway, things finally settled down. A union finally comes in. Every so often Ms. Lizzy comes and gets me at the mill and we talk by the river. We talked like this all the way up to the time her husband died.

"At the funeral with all them rich folks there, she leaves them all standing and walks to me and hugs me. She hugs me a long time and has been cryin. She told me right then she was gonna sell the mill. Don't know if she told anybody befo dat. It was a sad day for everybody, 'specially me."

"Have you heard from her since?" Jake asked.

"No sir."

"You can call me Jake."

"No, Jake."

The pleasant Carolina breeze continued to blow as the gum ball tree in the front yard gently swayed. "Can you think of anyone who might be trying to harass Ms. Lizzy. Someone who is a little unstable, or maybe has some sexual problems?" he asked.

"No sir. Jake, I mean. I's haven't heard anything. People I know wishes she was still here."

"She wanted me to give you her number. She said if you ever need anything or if you hear of anything that would be a help, to give her a call. She said there weren't many people she could trust with her number, but you were one that she could. Here is my card also."

Jake thanked her for her hospitality and headed back to Myrtle Beach.

CHAPTER 4

"Hello. Hey," Liz said as she cradled the phone. "Believe me I'm looking forward to a couple weeks in Edisto. Things have been crazy. I'll let you know when I see you. Okay, baby. I'll see you about 4. Bye."

Jerry Swanson was the current Lieutenant Governor of South Carolina and Republican candidate for U.S. Senate, not to mention Liz Alton's favorite squeeze. Fifty-four and a former all-American quarterback at Clemson, he had been a real comfort to Liz. They met three years before in Charleston at a Christmas party hosted by a mutual friend.

"Linda, I'll be calling on Tuesdays and Thursdays just to see how things are going. If you have any concerns at all call security or Jake Brown. You've got my Edisto number. Be sure the security alarm stays engaged at all times. You be very careful. You know how nervous I've been about all this stuff. I'll call Mr. Brown from Edisto tonight." Liz gave Linda a hug and grabbed her purse to leave.

"You have a good time, dear," Linda said as she squeezed Liz's hand. "You tell that hunk that he better treat you nice or I'm gonna get him. You tell him I said so." They embrace again as Liz headed out the door to begin the two-plus hour drive to Edisto.

Edisto Island had long been a favorite place for Liz Alton. Her late husband Harold had introduced her to it on their honeymoon. It was a great place to go and relax. There was not a single traffic light on the island. One of the main landmarks was a gas station. The island boasted seven or eight restaurants, a golf course and a couple of grocery stores. The wealthy and not so wealthy have enjoyed the privacy of Edisto for many years.

Her beach home was a beautiful structure built in the early seventies. It consisted of six bedrooms, a huge great room, and a large deck. She bought it three years ago. Liz could be just another person at Edisto, put on her sweats and relax.

Life had been good since she met Harold. She went from a struggling reporter to a millionaire's wife. It was certainly a dream move, but at times it had been difficult. Even though her life had mellowed out since the sale of the mill, this place still represented a place of refuge. With everything else going on, the "Welcome to Edisto" sign that greeted her was a very welcome sight.

After getting the basic supplies at the market, wine, beer, lunch meats and snacks, Liz arrived at the beach house about 2 p.m. She found the place just like she left it, perfect. She did have some concerns since at least two college weekend crowds had used the place since her last visit. Harold and Liz had not had any children but there were plenty of nieces and nephews. She was glad the kids could enjoy it. She got into her sweats, sipped some wine, grabbed a novel and relaxed in a recliner with a view of the ocean.

Jerry would be there in two hours. She wondered where this romance would lead. He seemed to be the perfect fit for her. They certainly clicked physically. They both had better conditioned bodies than most fifty-year olds. More than the physical though, they were friends. She never had to be someone else around Jerry. Up to this point they had not discussed marriage. Liz was old fashioned enough to hope that was where this thing was heading. She couldn't quite escape the guilt of their physical relationship without the commitment of marriage. Jerry had also expressed the same concerns. "This might just be when he pops the question," Liz mused. She contemplated what her response might be as she sipped her wine and stared at the broad expanse of the Atlantic Ocean.

Had she become overly paranoid about the harassment thing at home? She hoped that was the case. She picked up the phone and called Jake. After the recording answered she said, "Jake, this is Liz Alton. I will be at Edisto for a couple of weeks. You have my number here. I told Linda to call you if anything unusual happens. If you need to get in touch with me for any reason give me a call. Otherwise I'll talk to you when I get back. Thanks, bye."

"God, I love this place," she thought as she stretched out with her novel.

Jerry Swanson pulled in at 4:15 in his Suburban. The next three hours went as expected for a man and woman who liked each other, who thought they were in love, and who were definitely in heat. After Liz had about killed poor old Jerry, he emerged from the bedroom fresh from a shower and joined Liz in the living room.

"How ya doin' champ?" she smiled as she looked up from the paper.

"I feel like I've been knocked out in the third round," he said.

"I think it was the eighth round, and besides, the night is still young. You care for a beer?" she said heading for the refrigerator. She settled next to him a moment later with a frosted mug of beer for him. She laid her head on his broad shoulders. "I have missed you so much," Liz said.

Jerry caressed her soft shoulder and stroked her perfect blond hair. "Haven't got sick of me yet, huh?" Jerry said as he sipped his beer.

"Like I said, the night is young," Liz countered. "You gonna be our next Senator, or are all those reporters lying?"

"Well, it could happen, stranger things have happened in this state."

"You think so?"

"Well maybe not quite that strange," Jerry said. "If I get elected I guess I'll have to get me a residence in D.C. Maybe I can find one of those little college age aides to help keep my house tidy. Those girls tend to idolize Senators. What do you think?"

"I think you're full of it, that's what I think," Liz quipped. "If you think I kill you, one of those little sweethearts would finish the job. You might be over the hill but you're much too young to die."

"Yeah, and how would the undertaker ever get that big grin off my face?" Jerry said.

"Probably couldn't be done. I guess they'd have to bury you face down. Come to think of it, that might not be a bad idea."

"You mean like putting my best foot forward?" Jerry countered.

"Yeah, something like that," Liz replied.

Jerry got up, strolled to the window, and looked out over the ocean for several minutes. Liz slid her arms around from behind and nestled her man. "If I go to D.C. Liz, I want you to go with me. It has nothing to do with what people think. It has everything to do with the fact that I don't want to live apart from you." He turned to face her and cupped her pretty chin in his large hands. He stared into her adoring eyes and said, "I love you, Liz. I've always loved you."

She wiped the tears from his eyes and said, "I know, but thanks for saying it." She hugged him so tight she thought she might break him.

"I want to marry you, Liz. Will you have me?" Jerry asked.

~

Lenny Ragozzi the maintenance supervisor for Chesterfield Estates chewed on a toothpick as Shirley looked through the work orders for the day. Shirley was a bleached blond who enjoyed showing a lot of cleavage and wearing jeans just a little too tight. Her job monitoring the gate at Chesterfield was an easy job. Besides, she got to flirt with all the rich men who lived there and you better believe they all knew who she was. Part of her job was to keep track of the work orders for the maintenance crew.

"Adam Hoover said there was something wrong with his garage door and wanted it looked at today or tomorrow," she said. "Probably the best bet today is to go size up Liz Alton's place. She wanted some painting done while she was gone. Said she would be back in a couple weeks. The water main over on Russell Street still needs looked at."

Shirley looked at Lenny with a bored expression, void of any sign of intelligence. Seeing that no comment was forthcoming she commenced reading her magazine.

"Jerome, did you pick up that paint for the Alton job yet?" Lenny yelled to the next room.

"Yes sir, I sure did. Got seven gallons, five rollers, a new three-inch brush, and some putty. We are ready to proceed," Jerome Haze replied. Jerome was a twenty-nine-year-old black man who had been at Chesterfield from the beginning, even before they had any residences there. He was a hard worker and someone Lenny relied heavily upon. Jerome had a wife and two small children and was a devoted Christian man.

"Be a good day to get on it," Jerome continued. "Got nothing major staring at us, and besides, it's gonna take us several days to finish. She wants quite a bit done from what I understand."

Most of the time the crew had four workers. Lately Lenny had to make do with three, Jerome, Eddie Britain and himself. Eddie Britain had been with the crew a couple years. He was a good worker but was oftentimes moody and was not accused of being overly social. He was twenty-five years old with a tall athletic build, an olive complexion and dark hair. He lived with a girl named Jennifer of whom he rarely spoke. Sometimes he was a pain and more than once Lenny had threatened to let him go. But the guy showed up for work most of the time and in the maintenance game showing up was half the battle.

"We are off to the hunt. We will be at the Alton place all day," Lenny hollered at Shirley as she flipped him a quick wave and continued to flirt with a resident who just pulled up.

The maintenance truck pulled up to the Alton house at 9:15. Linda's car was the only one in the driveway. "We're here to do the painting, missy," Lenny said when Linda answered the door.

"Yes sir, Ms. Alton said to be expecting you," Linda answered as they drug in their stuff. "I guess she has shown you what she wants done—the hall, dining room and all the bedrooms?"

"She sure did. I expect this will take a few days. We should be done by Thursday," Lenny said as he directed Eddie to bring in a ladder and drop-cloth.

"You men just do what you need to do, I'll be about my business," Linda said as she scurried off.

The crew got busy with their work. Painting was one of their more common jobs. They were very careful when they had inside work to do in one of the Chesterfield homes. When something was broken in one of these places, it usually meant quite a sum of money, which had been known to come from the maintenance budget. Consequently, the men were very careful.

This job had special significance for Eddie Britain. Ms. Liz Alton had definitely caught his eye. One reason Eddie liked his job was he got to see all these rich ladies up close. Liz Alton was the finest looking one of all. Seeing her jog around the neighborhood in those spandex pants of hers was a sight he more than enjoyed. And here he was in the queen's domain.

Eddie had occasion to speak to her a time or two, once at the clubhouse and once when she jogged by the maintenance truck. Both times she just smiled and went her way. Eddie did not like to be brushed off by women. He wanted to be acknowledged. After all, he was a young, good-looking man. He could do these rich gals some good. Several in the complex could attest to that, but none half as good-looking as Liz. She needed to talk to Shirley to find out what she had been missing.

Eddie had a plan to bring the queen down. Shattering her nerves was a game with Eddie. He had been slow and deliberate, a little here, a little there. The cat, the panties, Eddie especially got off on that. The binoculars was a spur of the moment thing. The knife, he liked the knife.

The crew broke for lunch and came back around one. Eddie's afternoon job was to prep the master bedroom for painting. He was going to enjoy this. He routinely took time to look into the ladies' dresser drawers and was always particularly excited to see their exotic underwear. Eddie figured they weren't wearing this stuff for their husbands.

Discreetly looking through one of Liz's drawers, he spotted two black thongs. He slipped one into his pocket. He carefully replaced the other items and closed the drawer. "We don't want to leave a trail now do we?" Eddie thought.

"How's things looking in here?" Lenny asked as he stepped into the room. "We need to be finishing up soon. Looks like you got it ready to go. I'll put you on this room first thing tomorrow." Eddie nodded his head as Lenny left the room. "Things are definitely looking up," Eddie Britain said to himself. "The queen is coming down."

CHAPTER 5

Life for Jake Brown was getting back to normal. His trusty dog Amos had only messed on the floor once this week. Sally McSwain stopped by every day or so. Life was slow, the way Jake liked it. He didn't have any new developments on the Liz Alton mystery. The Georgetown trip was interesting but did not bring any new information. Liz was in Edisto and would not be back for another ten days. There was not much to do but just hang around. He wasn't complaining. Sounded like the retirement mode to him.

Walking onto the pier, Jake saw that things were a little testy. His fishing pal, Joe Lane, and the pier boss, Ralph, or "Bimbo," as Joe liked to refer to him, were in each other's face. Joe was holding what seemed to be blood worms in a plastic bag and was pointing at Ralph. Ralph was screaming and hopping mad.

"You stupid little jerk," Joe said, "See what trying to rob people will get you!"

"Give me that bait before I call the police," Ralph hollered.

"Call the police," Joe snarled, "I want to talk to a sane person!"

"At your service," Jake chimed in.

"My hero to the rescue!" Joe snarled as he marched toward the pier with the worms and yelled over his shoulder, "Up yours, Bimbo."

"I'm way too old to put up with his crap. Not a day goes by when he doesn't try to screw me out of something. How that wife of his puts up with him is beyond me," Ralph said. "I guess you want to fish?"

"I'm gonna try it for a little while anyway. Anything hitting?" Jake asked.

"A few spot are biting," Ralph said.

"And Joe screwed you out of some blood worms," Jake said with a sly smile.

"He's a bum," Ralph said. "Why you hang around with him I'll never know. The guy has zero class."

"I guess I'm a glutton for punishment."

"Guess so," he said handing Jake some blood worms and change, "Happy hunting." He turned to walk away and Ralph added, "Throw him in!"

The fishing was good. Jake fished for two hours and caught and cleaned twenty-third spot and a couple of whiting. Everybody was catching fish. When the fish were biting the action usually lasted several days and sometimes several weeks. Yes sir, it was a good time for a slow down in this private eye stuff. Jake decided he was going to come out here again tomorrow.

∼

Liz enjoyed the afternoon sun as the ocean breeze gently blew in her face. She loved watching Jerry fish. She felt a contentment with him that she had never known before. Her marriage to Harold had been a good one, but this was different. Jerry was closer to her age. They seemed to be on the same page. The thought of being Mrs. Jerry Swanson was a thought that warmed her heart. She had talked to Jerry at length about the odd events in her life. He felt she should move. More than likely it was just some neighborhood kids, but it could be worse. It was not worth the chance. He wanted her to move to Spartanburg so she would be close to him until the election and then they would be moving to Washington. Liz had always been a fighter and she did not like the idea of running. Besides, up to this point, all that had occurred were just idle threats, or maybe just coincidences.

Jerry placed his pole back in the holder sticking in the sand, had a seat next to Liz, and got a cold beer out of the cooler. "I got an idea," he said, "let's just live the rest of our lives at Edisto."

"That doesn't sound like a senator to me," Liz followed. "This place is a great get away, but all the time? I believe we would climb the wall," she said with an "ain't that so?" look.

He wondered how he could have been persuaded to run for the Senate. Being Lieutenant Governor was much more than he ever really wanted. But such is life. One thing seems to lead to another. "I think I could stand being a doting husband to this woman right here in Edisto," Jerry thought to himself. Turning back now, however, was not an option.

They made their plans. This wedding was not to be a media circus. They decided to get married at one of the instant wedding chapels in Myrtle Beach, just the two of them. They set the date for two weeks.

Liz loved Myrtle Beach. Jerry wanted her to sell the Chesterfield house but they would make that decision sometime in the future. She needed to be with her man. No doubt she could turn a nice profit on the house since real estate at the beach had been sky rocketing. A whole new chapter of her life was about to open and it sounded good to her.

On the way home Eddie Britain stopped at the Maze Gentleman's Club. He downed a few beers and enjoyed the entertainment. After leaving there he stopped at the store, picked up some beer and headed for home.

He lived with his girlfriend Jennifer on a dirt road about ten miles from the beach. It might as well be a million miles. It was a different world, filled with trees, bushes, swamp and snakes. Just the way he liked it.

Eddie met Jennifer two years ago. She had been a dancer at one of the clubs at the beach. She was into drugs and partying, a perfect match for Eddie. They had talked of getting hold of some money any way they could. Any way except the honest way that is. They talked about the money at Chesterfield. Eddie liked to talk about Liz Alton. She was the richest one of them all. He did not bother to tell Jennifer how good Liz looked. Some things are better left unsaid.

During one of their many grass and beer-filled evenings, Jennifer looked at Eddie and said, "We ought to kidnap that rich Alton bitch. I bet we could pull it off. What you think Eddie? Could we pull that off?"

Eddie thought for a few moments. The thought of having her captive was better than winning the lottery. "Anything is possible," he said.

"She owned that paper mill down there in Georgetown. She's got big time, old-school money," Jennifer pondered. "I saw in the paper that some wealthy big wig politician is her main man. I bet somebody would be willing to pay a lot of money to get her back. We really need to think on this Eddie.

We could make something happen. Now hand me that joint."

"I'm blessed, that's how I am, girl," Jerome Haze said to Linda. The Chesterfield maintenance crew was ready for another day of painting. "You need to meet my wife. She loves to sing in the choir. You would really like her."

"Did you meet her in Georgetown?" Linda asked.

"Sure did, high school sweetheart. Prettiest girl in South Carolina, too. My, my, the Lord sure has been good to me."

"Did you say that you attend Calvary Temple?"

"Sure do. Ooh, the Spirit in that place is so sweet. You need to come with us this Sunday. I mean it, sister. You need to meet my sweet wife, Donna."

"What time's the service?"

"Ten till whenever. I'm gonna save you a seat, girl," Jerome smiled, "You better be there now," he said as he headed down the hall with a drop-cloth singing "One Day at a Time Sweet Jesus."

Eddie went straight to Liz's bedroom. Jennifer had convinced him that kidnapping was the way to go. He thought about abducting her here. The problem with that was the security in this place was like Fort Knox. No money was spared. All of the latest security measures were in place. No, it would not be here. Somewhere not far away, however.

By mid-afternoon the following day the work at the Alton residence was completed. He would give it some time and then make his move.

The next few days were laid back for Jake Brown. The fishing was great at the Third Avenue Pier and Jake was able to fill his freezer with spot and whiting. Nothing new to report to Liz Alton. Jake talked to her every day or so just to keep in touch. She seemed much more at ease. Her time at Edisto was obviously doing her some good. Life was getting back to normal for everyone. Just another typical caper for Jake, except the money was a little greener.

Jake and Rudy Rogers got together and played golf at Homewood. And as usual, Rudy touched Jake for a few dollars. Life was good at Myrtle Beach.

~

On the second Thursday of November Jerry Swanson picked Liz Alton up at her place. It was about 1 in the afternoon. They drove into Myrtle Beach and went to a quickie wedding chapel on Highway 17. They paid the man seventy-five dollars and were married. As planned they went to a forty dollar a night motel on the beach and locked the door. Two days later they checked out.

Liz was not crazy about selling the house at the beach. She wanted to keep it as residence at least until Jerry won the senate seat. By all indications he certainly would win. Jerry was a conservative Republican in a state full of like-minded people. Having a warm personality and being a great orator certainly didn't hurt anything. He also had the backing of serious in-state money. After his marriage to Liz he went from your run of the mill multi-millionaire to one of the richest men in the state. To him she was the greatest thing since sliced bread. He would have married her even if she worked at a gas station. But the money certainly didn't hurt anything.

The first six months of the new year were busy for Liz and Jerry. Jerry had his duties as Lieutenant Governor, plus political rallies all over the state. He also had the whirlwind life of a newlywed.

They spent as much time together as they could. Their time was split between Spartanburg and Myrtle Beach. When together, they were clinging to each other like a couple of college kids. When apart, Jerry was campaigning and Liz was busy planning the décor of their Washington mansion. They were the darlings of the state. Everyone was thrilled with their union. Jerry, an already strong candidate, now with Liz at his side, truly seemed unbeatable.

As winter turned to spring, and spring turned to summer, Liz forgot about her past harassment, or imagined harassment. It had been seven or eight months since anything strange had happened. Life was finally getting to where Liz could again feel comfortable.

She contacted Jake and told him that she felt things had blown over. If anything new came up she would be in touch. She paid him much more money than he expected. He felt guilty taking it. Oh well, the old truck could use a paint job.

Jake resumed his anemic private eye business with a couple of "trail my old man" cases. Life was slow and Jake wasn't complaining.

CHAPTER 6

June in Myrtle Beach was a great time to be in the tourist business. People from all over the eastern U.S. and Canada head for the Golden Strand. It was a time when money was made and hearts were broken.

The first week of June found Liz at her Chesterfield residence. Jerry was in Greenville campaigning. She was expecting him home in two days. Their life together had been all she expected.

Tuesday evening was very warm. Thank God the breeze from the ocean made things bearable. Liz was a devoted fan of exercise and liked to jog in the neighborhood. Summertime jogging could only be done early in the morning or in the evening. It was just too hot any other time. She was out for such a jog this warm summer evening. She wore short spandex running pants, a Clemson Athletic Dept. t-shirt, and a ball cap. After running for about thirty-five minutes she had worked up a good sweat. She ran the same path everyday covering about three miles. After her run she would walk the last half-mile home to cool down.

Exercise was one of the things that Liz made herself do. She did it for herself and for Jerry. After finishing her run she slowed to an even slower than usual walk on this warm summer night. She loved living at Chester-field. She would have to find a way to convince Jerry to keep the house.

Liz was a creature of habit. On summer evenings when a thunderstorm wasn't eminent, Liz would stop at the same creek on an isolated stretch of the road. The creek was one half mile from home and she would usually go down the bank and stand and watch the life in the marsh. It was a nice way to reflect at the end of the day.

She didn't see Eddie Britain in the brush behind her. They were half a mile from any other human beings. Eddie secretly gazed at Liz in her tight charcoal gray spandex shorts. He was not more than twenty feet from her.

His plan was to rush her and grab her before she could scream.

He had to move fast. He lunged for her. She heard something at the last second but it was too late. As she turned to see her attacker he was already on her throwing her to the ground. Rage and lust filled the man's eyes. She knew she'd seen him somewhere before, but where? Eddie sprawled out on top of her and covered her mouth so she couldn't scream. She tried to bite him and kick him but she couldn't. He was too strong.

He wrapped duct tape around her mouth. Her adrenaline was flowing but so was his. She could not escape. He wrapped her hands and feet. She was helpless. Eddie dragged her under the bridge and tied her to a cable that ran from the bridge. She was paralyzed with fear. Eddie ran his rough hands all over her body and under her clothing. "We're gonna get to know each other real well baby. Real well," Eddie hissed.

Eddie looked up and down the road and nothing was coming. He quickly walked the four hundred yards up the road to get his car. It was parked in a maintenance turn off out of sight from the road. He pulled the Buick down to the bridge where Liz was bound. Being sure that no one was coming, he stepped out and opened the trunk. He went down the bank and manhandled her in to the trunk. She was completely bound and gagged.

Eddie got in the car and drove out of the development with no more than a nod from the college kid at the gate. He headed for home. The wealthiest woman in South Carolina was trapped in the trunk of a maniac's car.

Between gasps of breath, Liz Swanson prayed for her life.

It was 6:15 when Eddie pulled into his drive. Jennifer was standing at the door looking his way. The grin on Eddie's face told her that things had gone well.

Eddie got out and opened the trunk of the car. His eyes met Liz's terror filled eyes. He threw her over his shoulder and headed for the lot behind the trailer. Seventy-five yards behind the trailer was a forty-by-forty dog lot, complete with five vicious rottweilers.

In the middle of the lot was a ten-foot by ten-foot soundproof cinder block building. The building was built with double cinder blocks and six inches of insulation between the blocks. They wanted to be sure that no sound could be heard over the sound of the dogs barking. They had accomplished their task.

Jennifer opened the gate to the dog lot. The dogs did not run out since they had been trained to stay in the fence. She closed the gate as Eddie carried Liz inside the dog lot. Jennifer opened the door of the building, and they went inside.

The furnishings consisted of a small bed, a bucket with water in it, another bucket for a commode, a candle lantern, a small three-drawer dresser, and a straight back wooden chair.

Once inside, Jennifer lit the candles as Eddie laid Liz on the bed.

"What you think of that?" asked Eddie.

"I think we're gonna have a lot of fun out here. You didn't tell me she was so good looking. I'm gonna enjoy this girl, Eddie, I really am," Jennifer said as her eyes lusted over Liz.

"Tell me about it, darling," Eddie said as he unwrapped the tape from Liz's feet and hands. He stripped her from the waist down and shackled her feet to the bed. Jennifer and Eddie hovered over their terrified victim.

"Please don't," Liz whispered. "Please don't do this to me. I'll give you money, whatever you want," she pleaded.

"We know you will, baby. We know you will," Eddie smiled. "You're in our world now, sugar. We really aren't all that nice. And you know what? I don't really care about your money. We're just gonna enjoy your company for a while," Eddie smiled as Jennifer pulled her tank top off.

He did care about the money. They both did, but not tonight and probably not for a while. They had what they wanted.

"Yeah honey, you're gonna be my new girlfriend, and Eddie's too. Now don't that sound nice?" Jennifer said as her eyes danced over Liz's trembling body. "Take that old stuffy t-shirt and bra off, baby. It's much too hot tonight. Don't you think?" Jennifer purred. "You're gonna find out soon enough that you will have to cooperate. You don't want us to have to hurt you now, do you? Take it off!" she ordered.

In sheer terror Liz pulled off her shirt and bra.

Eddie and Jennifer poured out their lust upon Liz for what seemed like an eternity. She tried to block out the terrible things that were happening to her. With every passing second her crippled self-esteem dropped even farther into a cavern that she had never known or imagined. For the first time in her life Liz wished with all her might that she would die. If it were in her power she would.

They were right about one thing. She was definitely in their world now. She felt such a rage for these two animals that she could kill them without any twinge of conscience. She prayed to God that she would have that chance.

Sometime in the middle of the night, Eddie and Jennifer went back to the trailer and left Liz to weep alone.

Later in the night Liz fell asleep. She did not know how long she slept. There was no way of telling since there were no windows and the only light was the faint hint of daylight from a vent pipe that wound around overhead. She could tell it was daytime but that was all. There was just enough light to allow her to see a candle and some matches next to the bed. She sat up in bed and lit the candle. She was sickened as she recalled the terror of the previous night. "When will they be back?" she thought. She noticed her clothes were gone. The only garment in the room, was a small pair of black panties lying on the table with a note attached to them. It read, "This is your wardrobe. Put them on. I'll be very disappointed if you don't have them on when I see you tonight. Love, Eddie." She shuddered as she read the note.

Also on the table sat a small container of peanuts, a tomato, and a pack of crackers. Liz noticed the bucket of water with a towel and soap next to it. She also noticed the other bucket and rightly figured this was her latrine.

The only sounds she heard were the occasional bark or growl from one of the dogs. The tight insulation blocked any sound of birds, wind, or anything else.

Liz cleaned herself up and used the pee pot. After she had some peanuts and a cracker she sat down in her bed and cried like she had never cried before.

CHAPTER 7

Linda pulled into the drive at Chesterfield at 9:15. She went around back and pulled the trash buggy to the curb just like she did every Wednesday morning. "It's gonna be another hot one," she said to herself. Linda thought how thankful she was that she could work in this beautiful, comfortable environment for a sweet lady like Liz. She was so happy for Liz and Jerry. They were in love. She smiled as she unlocked the front door and walked in.

The house was unusually still. There was no smell of coffee and no sign of Liz. "Ms. Lizzy," Linda called. There was no answer. "How strange," Linda thought. She went to the master bedroom. The bed looked just like Linda had made it the morning before. There was still no sign of Liz. "Ms. Lizzy?" Linda called again.

Linda noticed in the bedroom that the closet door was open and Liz's jogging shoes were not there. "Maybe she went for a jog," she thought. "She'll be home soon, it's getting too hot out there."

She walked into the kitchen to make coffee and noticed the answering machine had three unanswered calls on it. She pressed the play button. They were all from Jerry. He called the previous evening at 7:25 and 9:40, and this morning at 8:25. The call this morning sounded full of worry and concern.

Linda dialed Jerry's Spartanburg phone number. He answered on the second ring.

"Hello," he answered.

"Jerry, this is Linda. I noticed you called. She's not here. I'm a little concerned. The bed doesn't look like its been slept in. Her jogging shoes are gone. I'm hoping she's jogging somewhere. If so she should be coming in soon. It's getting hot."

"Strange," Jerry said, "She doesn't usually jog this late in the morning. Is there anything else out of place?"

"No, everything seems normal. Everything but the bed that is. That's very strange."

"You're sure it hasn't been slept in?"

"Absolutely."

"I think I better come in. I'll leave here in a few minutes. I should be there by 2. Call my cell phone number if there is any news." Jerry hung up the phone, called his secretary and told her to cancel his appointments. He was on the road within ten minutes.

The only concept of time that Liz could detect was the heat. The building itself was fairly cool being made from block, plus it was located in the shade. She noticed it was getting a little warmer as time went on. Eventually she got up from the bed and looked over her prison. It was very solid, almost completely airtight. Any sounds from the outside were very muted. The furnishings were meager indeed.

She figured she must be missed by now. It was probably a little early for them to call the authorities. Sometime today that would certainly change. Liz figured the ride from the beach took about a half-hour. It was obvious that she was in a remote location.

Her body ached from the relentless and terrible attack of the night before. From her thighs to her lips she had been terribly abused. A gasp and shudder came to Liz with every thought of the terrible ordeal. What more could those two animals do to her?

Apart from the physical assault the mental assault would be the main battle she had to win. She had always been the strong one. Even as a child from a good home in Missouri, Liz always was the one her brothers and sister gained strength from. As a child she always felt a responsibility toward her siblings since she was the oldest of four. Not once had she let them down. She was always the one whose emotional state was not dictated by circumstances. This would be the ultimate challenge of her life. Whether she lived or died she would not surrender her soul to these people. She would die with emotional dignity if it came to that.

Her heart broke for her husband Jerry. He so adored her. So much was on him, and now this. She hung her head and cried for her husband. She missed him terribly. Even in the midst of terrible circumstances she put others ahead of herself. She bowed her head and prayed.

~

Jerry arrived at Victor Lane about 2 p.m. Linda met him as he walked to the door. Her appearance conveyed that good news was not forthcoming. As he approached the door his asking eyes were met by the sad shaking of her head. He walked directly to Liz's bedroom not saying a word.

"My God, Liz, where are you?" he said half to himself. He sat down on the bed, and buried his face in his hands. Linda stood at the door, frozen by the moment. "God, please send her home to me," Jerry said.

After several minutes Jerry rose, went to the phone, and dialed 911. A moment later he was connected to Bertha at the Myrtle Beach Police Department. Thirty minutes later Sergeant Rudy Rogers was knocking at his door.

"Mr. Swanson? I'm Officer Rogers."

"Please come in and have a seat," Jerry said pointing the way. "I'm very worried about my wife. This is so unlike her. She just would not go off without telling someone."

"I see. When was the last time anyone actually saw her?" Rudy asked.

"Linda saw her yesterday afternoon about 5. That's when she leaves," Jerry said looking toward Linda.

"Did you notice anything unusual?" the officer asked Linda.

"No sir, she was in such a good mood. She was looking forward to Mr. Swanson coming home later in the week."

"As far as you know was she planning on going anywhere or was she expecting anyone?"

"Not a thing. I'm sure she was planning to jog. She did that most every night," Linda said.

"Does she jog here in the development?" Rudy asked.

"She always runs here."

"You told me on the phone her jogging shoes were missing. Is that correct?"

"Yes sir," Linda said. "When I came in this morning I noticed the closet door ajar and her shoes were gone. I assumed she was jogging."

"Did she always run the same route?"

"I think so, as far as I know," Linda said.

"Did she ever mention to either one of you where she might run?"

Jerry thought for a moment, "I think she runs the perimeter. Royal Drive circles the complex. I know she usually runs for about thirty minutes. Then she walks the last ten or fifteen minutes home to cool down."

"Was that also on Royal Drive?"

"I don't think so, she usually walks down Shady Lane on the way home. It's not developed yet. She likes to stop at the creek there and watch the birds. It gives her a chance to be quiet," Jerry Swanson said with alarm in his eyes.

Several neighbors watched the house with great interest. A police car in this neighborhood always meant theft.

"Could we ride the route she probably jogged?" Rudy asked.

"Sure, let's go," Jerry said as he and Officer Rogers headed out the door.

Sometime towards evening, Liz heard the rattling of the door lock. Eddie Britain walked in. The candle was burning and he clearly saw Liz sitting in the chair. He walked over to her and lifted her trembling head up. "Stand up let me see," he said as he stepped back and admired her thong attire. "Now don't you look fine," he said as he began to disrobe.

After two hours of assault, Eddie secured Liz's hands to the headboard and her feet to the straps on the side of the bed. He left with a wink.

Twenty minutes later Jennifer arrived. She had fresh water with her, several washcloths, a towel, toothpaste, deodorant, and some more food.

"A woman's work is never done," Jennifer said. She emptied the slop bucket, and held the door open for a few minutes. "This place is a little stuffy, don't you think, sugar?" she smiled. "I'm gonna talk to Eddie about giving you a little fresh air. I'm the only friend you got now," she said as she sat down next to Liz and began to sponge her body in a sensual manner.

An hour later Eddie arrived. He undid the straps and they left, leaving Liz to weep.

Chapter 8

Thursday morning arrived with no sign of Liz. She was officially a missing person. Rudy Rogers and Deputy Larry James headed for Chesterfield. Rudy liked to work with Deputy James. He was an easy-going southern fellow with high morals and a good sense of humor.

They pulled into Chesterfield and Shirley approached them at the gate. She was in her usual glory, form-fitting jeans and a shirt with two thirds of the buttons undone. "I love men in uniform," she said as she looked in the patrol car window.

"Yes ma'am," Rudy said as he tipped his hat. "We've got some business here today."

This got Shirley's attention, "Who you going to see?"

"I'd rather not say right now," Rudy said knowing darn well she'd know within the hour. "Do you stop every car that comes through?" Rudy asked.

"Just the men," she smiled. Rudy could definitely believe that. "You guys looking for a bad guy?"

"Maybe. What time do you leave?"

"Eight to four," she said shifting from her flirt mode to her dumb blond routine. She was starting to feel a little defensive. Her job included logging every car that came through the gate. Which, of course, was something she never did, unless it was some man's cell phone number.

"We'll be in touch," Sergeant Rogers said as they drove off.

Shirley hustled inside, radioed maintenance supervisor Lenny Ragozzi and told him something was up. He would be sure to get the scoop.

The mood at the Swanson estate was terribly depressing and going down hill by the minute. Jerry Swanson had already called the South Carolina Republican Party Headquarters and told them that all things were on hold. Every dream and every aspiration was empty without Liz.

In so many ways Jerry Swanson had lived a blessed life. But he didn't really know what blessed was until he met Liz. Now his world was crumbling about him.

He couldn't help but feel guilty. Liz was so worried about the strange things that were happening. They seemed like childish acts to him—just pranks that adolescents play. Could they be connected to her disappearance? Only time would tell.

The general consensus of opinion was that Liz had probably been abducted during her evening jog. Most likely it had occurred in the undeveloped section of Shady Lane. The police were scouring that area looking for any possible clues. The neighbors were all asked if they had seen anything or anybody suspicious. Not a thing had come up.

At 1:15 Lenny Ragozzi led Sergeant Rudy Rogers into his maintenance security office.

Lenny's office was surprisingly nice with fresh paint and a new carpet. It even had a new couch and armchair. Rudy expected that Shirley frequented that couch from time to time. That would be accurate. "Do you have a record of the people who came through the gate Tuesday?" Rudy asked.

"We have an incomplete list," Lenny said knowing full well that Shirley had one thing and one thing only on her mind, and it wasn't job performance.

"Could I see it?"

"Certainly," Lenny went to the next room and took the register from Shirley. "You are going to get your act together and I mean soon," Lenny growled to Shirley. "And tomorrow I want you dressing like a professional instead of some damn slut." Evidently Lenny had slept through his political correctness classes. "Here it is," he said handing it to Rudy.

The record was not impressive. A total of eight entries were made. On any given hour at least fifteen cars went by. "Could I talk to her," Rudy said motioning toward Shirley.

"Sure. Shirley, could you step in here?" Lenny said loudly. "The poor girl could sure use a job at the police department. What ya think, Sarge?"

"I don't think so."

"Have a seat," Lenny said as Shirley walked in. "Officer Rogers want to ask you a few questions."

"I noticed your entries here. I'm sure this is only a partial list of the cars. Is that right?"

"Yes officer. I guess I let a few go by."

"Do you remember anything unusual Tuesday?"

"No sir, same old stuff. Nothing sticks out," she said chewing her gum like there was no tomorrow.

"You told me earlier that you get off at four. Is that right?"

"Yes sir."

"Who comes on then?"

"Tuesday night it was Harold."

"And Harold is?"

"Harold is a college kid we just hired. He goes to Coastal Carolina," Lenny said. "Good kid. Right now he works Tuesday and Friday nights."

"So he comes in at four?"

"Right."

"So he'll be in tomorrow? I need to talk to him before that. I'll get his number before I leave."

"Catching that boy home won't be an easy trick. I have to call all day to get up with him. Doesn't believe in answering machines," Lenny said.

"That'll be all, Shirley. Thank you." She wasted no time in leaving.

"Who hangs around this place enough to know people's habits?"

"Other than the residents? No one I can think of. This just isn't the kind of place where people spy on one another. These people are much too busy to worry about what anyone else is doing."

"What about your crew?"

"What about 'em?"

"Tell me about your people."

Lenny Ragozzi looked at Rudy with hard eyes, "They're good boys. You don't have to worry about them."

"Were they here past five on Tuesday?"

"Half the time we don't get out of here till past five, sometimes six."

"Tell me about your boys."

"He's a pushy S.O.B.," Lenny thought. "I got two boys now, Jerome Haze and Eddie Britain. Two of the best workers I've ever had. In fact,

Jerome has been with me since we shoveled our first pile of dirt here. Very good man, Christian man. Eddie's a good boy. Quiet, but he shows up every day and does his job, and in this business that's worth a lot."

"I'd like to talk to them."

"I'll call them in now if you want me to."

"What time do you expect them in?"

"About four."

"I'll talk to them then," Rudy said. "Thanks for your time, I'll be back at four." Rudy met up with Deputy James and they headed out for a burger and coke.

Overwhelming helplessness haunted Jerry Swanson. Few times in his life had he felt helpless. Not since Vietnam when, as a young Lieutenant, he watched fifteen of his best men die over the course of two months somewhere in Cambodia. They were men under his command, men who looked to him. This was his wife. He had yet to call family and friends because he hoped she would show up. He would give it a few more hours then make some calls.

He racked his brain over what might have happened. Was there anyone who was the least bit suspicious? His mind drew a blank. He prayed that she was still alive. And if she were still alive, would he find her?

The word spread like wildfire around Chesterfield. Liz seemingly had been abducted. This enclave of the rich was given a gripping reality check. All were nervous, many were angry. They paid a premium price for so-called security. Like the rest of the world, they were learning there were no guarantees. Security technicians and realtors would be facing busy and profitable days ahead.

Linda, the maid at the Swanson house, busied herself with routines she always did. Watering the flowers, dusting, doing laundry, preparing meals. She worked and prayed the afternoon away.

"I want you to continue, Linda. No matter how this turns out," Jerry said. "You know this place much better than I do. Frankly, I don't know how I'd manage without you." Leaning against the kitchen counter, he stared into the glass of ice water he had just prepared. "What are we going to do?" he asked.

"We're gonna pray and trust God. That's what we're gonna do," replied Linda as she prepared lunch.

"I've never been much at praying."

"First time for everything," she said.

"Isn't that the truth," Jerry thought to himself. "Isn't that the truth."

Rudy Rogers and Larry James got up with the crime scene boys who were checking the jogging trail for any kind of lead. Nothing out of the ordinary showed up. Larry interviewed some of the neighbors and Rudy went back to the gatehouse to talk to the maintenance crew.

Eddie Britain was the first to step into Lenny's office. He was alone with Sergeant Rogers.

"My name is Sergeant Rogers. Please have a seat," Rudy said extending his hand and motioning for him to sit down. "Eddie Britain, is that right?"

"That's right," Eddie said. "Just relax," he kept telling himself.

"I'm sure you're familiar with the alleged abduction of Mrs. Swanson?"

"Yes sir."

"Have you had an opportunity to meet her?"

"No sir. I've seen her around."

"Around how, walking, driving, what?"

"Both. She drove a silver Lexus and she jogged quite often."

"When did she usually jog?"

"Most of the time I saw her was in the evenings."

"Anything in particular you could say about her?"

"Well, she was good looking. She looked good jogging. That's kind of hard to miss." Nice touch Eddie thought. "I usually don't miss that kind of thing," smiled Eddie.

Rudy gave him a knowing nod, "Lenny told me you sometime work till five or six. Is that right?"

"Yes sir."

"What time did you get off Tuesday evening?"

Eddie thought for a moment, "I don't know . . . I guess about 5:30 or so."

"Do you remember what you were doing after five on Tuesday?"

"We'd been doing some yard work that day. Sometimes I make a final check to be sure we didn't leave anything laying around in the yard."

"Where did you go?"

"I checked a couple of houses on Hawthorn Drive."

"Did you see Liz Swanson jogging that evening?" Rudy asked. Several neighbors had concurred that Liz had been seen jogging along Royal Drive sometime around 5:30.

"No I didn't," Eddie said.

"Can you think of anyone who would want to harm Liz Swanson?"

"Nobody I know of," answered Eddie Britain.

"I guess you live in the area?"

"Yes sir, I live south of Conway about twelve miles."

"How long have you been there?" Sergeant Rogers asked.

"A little over two years. Before that I lived in Georgetown," Eddie volunteered.

"I hope you understand our concern. A missing person is a very serious thing. We have to check anyone and everyone who knew her or who knew of her habits. Consequently, all the employees here will remain suspects until we prove otherwise," Rudy said as he looked over his glasses. "We'll be in touch. Send Mr. Haze in please, and thank you for your time."

Eddie rose and nodded as he left the room.

The interview with Jerome Haze went along the same lines. He also sometimes worked until 6. On Tuesday he also left sometime after five. He did not know of anyone who had any intention to harm Liz Swanson. He agreed with Eddie that she was a striking woman who was well liked in the development. After fifteen minutes, Rudy thanked him for his time and everyone called it a day.

Chapter 9

Jake Brown was enjoying the good life—fishing, golf, female friends, and good health. He'd certainly be starving if he had to depend on the private eye business. The occasional nickel-and-dime cases he managed to luck into were usually a nice diversion. The pocket change they brought in came in handy.

Jake spent the morning fishing at the pier and the afternoon shopping with Sally. That evening he turned into the Meadows development and drove to his home on Palmer Street.

Amos was going wild in the back yard as Jake picked up the paper and the mail and meandered into the house. "This house smells like dog," he thought to himself as he opened the door. There were no messages on the answering machine. Jake opened the back door and Amos bounded in. Grabbing a cold one, he sat down to look at the paper.

He sprayed beer all over his pants and Amos when he saw Liz's picture plastered across the front-page with the headline, "Liz Swanson Missing— Believed Abducted from Chesterfield Estates." Jake barely breathed as he read the article. "My God," he said as he read it again. The paper said that Rudy Rogers was heading up the local investigation. He dialed Rudy's number.

Rudy had just walked in the door when Jake called. Fortunately Jake was the first one to call. The ringer on the phone was about to be turned off. Rudy gave Jake all the information he felt comfortable giving a jack leg private eye. They talked about ten minutes and made plans to play golf the following week.

Jake settled into his chair deep in thought. "It must be the same guy who was pulling those pranks," he reasoned. He wondered if she were still alive, and if she were, what was she going through?

Eddie Britain arrived home about 6. His mind raced as he entered the trailer. "Things are starting to heat up," he announced to Jennifer who was sprawled out on the sofa in her gym shorts and tank top.

"Let me guess, the fuzz have arrived?"

"Big time," Eddie said. "They asked me some questions a couple of hours ago."

Jennifer quickly sat up and said, "You're kidding?"

Eddie shook his head and walked to the refrigerator, "Not kidding," he said, "They interviewed everyone, Lenny, Shirley, Jerome."

"How did it go?"

"I don't think they're suspicious. . . .The cop said that we would all remain suspects, whatever that means."

"You think they'll come out here snooping around?"

"They might. If they do they won't mess with the dogs. They won't look in the lot."

"What if they do?" Jennifer asked.

"We're screwed that's what." Eddie sat down in his chair and stared out the front door. "Cops were crawling all over that place today. There was a whole crew of people checking along Shady Lane too. That's where I grabbed the bitch."

"You think they found anything? Did you leave any evidence?"

"What do you think? I sure as hell ain't gonna leave something just laying around. It's got me a little paranoid though. I've been thinking about the place where I pulled the car in. The ground was solid but maybe they can match a tire print. I just don't know."

"Why didn't you think of that?" Jennifer snapped. "You should have parked on the road."

"I couldn't take that chance. She might have gotten suspicious," Eddie said with his hands on his hips as he walked to the door. "I'm goin' into Conway to get some tires. I'll get used ones. New ones would be to obvious."

"You better do it now."

Eddie shook his head in agreement and headed out the door.

～

Liz had spent another despairing day. Physically sore and emotionally bankrupt from the two previous nights, she stared at the dim light from above. She could tell it was getting toward evening. They would certainly be back. Probably just like the night before, Eddie first, then Jennifer. She was sick to her stomach, but Lord she didn't want to throw up. The smell would be awful. The ventilation left everything to be desired. The thought of Eddie abusing her body was terrible beyond belief. She had to cooperate. He made that very clear. The guilt from submitting was tormenting. The consequences for not submitting would certainly be worse.

Sometime after sundown Eddie arrived followed later by Jennifer. Liz cried herself to sleep again.

～

The following morning Jake gave Amos a dog bone and a pat on the head. He put him in the back lot and headed out to the truck. A few minutes later he pulled into the Beach Deli and grabbed a seat by the window as Jill Arthur brought him coffee.

"Here you go, baby. You need some sugar?" she said with a wink.

"God, if you only knew," Jake said. She smiled and waited on a man at the counter. A few minutes later she brought him a sausage biscuit. "How'd you know I wanted that?" Jake said.

She put her hand on her hip and said, "You want me to take it back?"

"I don't think so," he said after the first bite. She moved on to talk to a table of construction workers who were having a testosterone attack.

Jake finished his breakfast and headed toward the door. He grabbed Jill's elbow and said, "The Bahamas are nice this time of year."

"Talk's cheap, Jake," she said as she swatted him on the rear with the menu as he went out the door.

～

At 9:45 Friday morning the Swanson residence was buzzing with activity. Jake pulled to a stop in front of the house. He started to lock his old truck but decided that the Chesterfield crowd was not quite that hard up for wheels.

The property was crowded with vehicles. Two police cars, three dark blue government sedans, a few cars he didn't recognize, and three TV crew trucks were scattered about. Linda was sweeping the front porch when Jake came up. "Ma'am, Jake Brown, Strand Private Eye," he said extending his hand.

"Yes, Mr. Brown," she said in her usual gracious manner.

"I am so sorry," Jake said. Linda's eyes told the whole story as she nodded her head in acknowledgement.

"I had to get out of there. It's been a zoo around here," she said. "Could I get you some tea, Mr. Brown?"

"Yes, thank you, and call me Jake. I guess Officer Rogers is here?"

"He sure is. Come on in and have a seat, I'll get him for you."

"Thank you, Linda," he said. Jake wandered in and sat in the very same chair where he sat when he first talked to Liz.

Several important-looking men went in and out of the door carrying brief cases containing audio and video equipment.

"How'd you get in here?" Rudy asked as he walked into the room.

"Blame Linda, she likes me."

"And she seems like such a nice girl too," Rudy said. "These FBI pukes would have you put in federal prison if they knew you were here."

"I hope they don't see my truck."

"Yeah, maybe they're blind."

"So what's happening?" Jake said.

"Nobody's got a clue. The Feds showed up today. They're a little put out with me. I didn't pucker up and kiss their ass when they walked in here. See that clown over there?" Rudy said pointing to a man in the hall. "Homer Southard, lead man for the FBI. The guy's a jerk."

"He does seem a little overbearing," Jake noted.

"You could say that. I guess I should be glad they're here. We need all the help we can get."

Jerry Swanson came into the room and said, "Rudy, I've got to go into town for about an hour. You have my cell phone number?" Rudy nodded that he did. "I don't believe I've had the pleasure," Jerry said extending his hand toward Jake.

Jake stood and said, "Jake Brown, Strand Private Eye."

"Jake Brown. Liz thought very highly of you."

"I can't tell you how sorry I am, Mr. Swanson."

"Thank you. You got any ideas?"

"I wish I did, sir. We're just comparing notes."

"I don't care how you do it in New York," FBI agent Homer Southard hollered over his shoulder as he barged into the room. Homer was a short, balding, pot-bellied, angry bureaucrat. "We're gonna interview everyone in the complex, all the workers, everybody," he said.

"We've already done that. You want to look at what we got?" Sergeant Rogers said.

Homer did not seem to hear him. "And who are you?" he growled at Jake.

Jake extended his hand, "Jake Brown, Strand Private Eye."

"Get him out of here. Now!" Homer screamed.

Jerry Swanson grabbed Homer's hunched shoulders, swung him around and said, "Mr. Brown is here because I asked him to be here and I would appreciate your acting like you have just a little bit of sense."

"No problem," Homer said as he charged out the door in pursuit of his next victim.

"And I thought I wanted to go to Washington," Jerry said as he grabbed his hat. "I'll be back in about an hour. Call me if anything comes up. It's very nice to meet you, Jake. Feel free to come by any time. I'll take care of that little prick."

"My pleasure sir, and thank you."

Linda brought Jake some tea and left Rudy and Jake alone. "Do you have any ideas, Jake?"

Jake shook his head no and said, "I can't help but think that the stuff going on before is somehow related to this. She was not a flaky person. She's very balanced. This is not the kind of neighborhood where you would find people who get off on tricks like that. She was dealing with someone strange."

"If those instances were related then whoever it was, was here on several occasions. That tells me it probably was someone who would not raise any suspicions going or coming around here," Rudy said.

"A resident you think?"

"That or a worker. There's plenty of maintenance and service people coming in and out of here. Everybody's got plenty of domestic help. Probably two or three hundred initial suspects."

"I guess you've talked to the workers here?"

"Talked to them yesterday. Pretty typical bunch, no red flags that I could see. I'm sure the Fed boys will dig some more."

"Mr. Swanson seems like a great guy. I heard he may drop out of the race for Senate."

"If this thing doesn't break soon, I'm sure he will," Rudy said.

Jake and Rudy chatted for several more minutes. Jake said goodbye and headed home. Rudy had one more stop to make.

Harold Miller worked the gatehouse the night that Liz was supposedly abducted. Twenty years old and a student at Coastal Carolina, he enjoyed the Chesterfield job because it gave him time to read and do his studies. Rudy was unable to get up with him until he reported for work on Friday evening.

"Harold," Rudy said as he extended his hand. "I'm Sergeant Rogers with the Myrtle Beach Police Department. I guess you've heard about this mess with Liz Swanson?"

"Who hasn't heard of it? It's on all the channels."

"I'm sure you've given some thought to the people who were coming and going through the gate that evening, especially between 4:30 and 6?"

"I keep a log," Harold said.

"Do you have it now?"

"Sure," he said handing a spiral notebook to Rudy.

"Is this all the evening traffic?"

"Everything except the ducks that come through every hour or so."

"At last, something to go on," Rudy thought. Harold had carefully noted who it was and what time they had passed through the gate. It was just the kind of record that Shirley was supposed to keep, but of course she was too busy hustling every man she saw to do her job. Most of the entries were the residents or their guests. Three or four service contractors were also recorded leaving the complex. One television repair vehicle arrived at 4:10 and left at 6:10. Rudy took note. He also noticed Eddie Britain left at five forty that evening, Jerome at 5:20.

"I really appreciate your diligence in doing your job," Rudy said to Harold. "I need to make a copy of this," he said referring to the notebook. "Was there anything unusual that stuck out in your mind that evening?" Rudy asked.

"Not really. I've tried to think of everything. I just don't have a clue."

"Anyone around here that you would consider a suspicious person?"

Harold thought for a moment. "Not really. They all seem pretty straight shooting to me."

"Would you say it's unusual for Eddie Britain to be working as late as he did?"

"Not really. The maintenance guys are sometimes here until 10."

"No one looked suspicious as they went by the gate?" Rudy said fishing.

"Not a thing," Harold said.

"Is there any chance you could have missed anyone?"

"I guess it's possible. I might have made a nature call. I just don't remember."

Rudy made a few copies of the notebook, thanked Harold for his time, and called it a day.

Chapter 10

Eddie arrived home about 6 p.m. He found Jennifer in her usual skimpy attire. He was not in a good mood.

Walking in, he grabbed a beer and sat down. Jennifer knew better than to bug him. After twenty minutes of silence, Eddie said, "The big boys arrived today, the FBI. They talked to Lenny. I'm sure they're gonna ask me some questions soon. We got to figure out a plan. If not, they're gonna find out." Jennifer didn't say anything. Eddie continued, "I think we need to send a ransom letter."

"Aren't you forgetting something?" Jennifer said. Eddie gave her that "tell me already look." She continued, "She knows who you are. We cannot just turn her over to them. She just might talk."

"Brains are definitely not your strong suit. That's exactly why I think we should send a ransom note. They would have to figure it's someone she doesn't know."

"That's good thinkin, Eddie."

Eddie shook his head in agreement. Any financial payoff would have to come later. Right now they had to get the Feds off their tail. Besides, he was enjoying the side benefits. "We have to be careful how we do the note. It can't be handwritten. It needs to be mailed from out of the area."

"I can do it on my typewriter," she said.

"I didn't know you had one."

"Under my bed," she said.

They spent the next hour formulating a letter. They had dinner, downed a couple beers and went to see Liz.

Liz heard them coming. The dogs made a certain kind of sound when they showed up. Hate was a new emotion to Liz. She was not sure what they really wanted with her. It didn't make sense if it was just sex. She was no spring chicken. It's got to be the money. "I've got to be smarter than these two," Liz said to herself as they both came in. They both started to disrobe and her nightmare continued.

Liz was awakened by the small light change that came with the dawn. Her body ached from the assault of the night before. Eddie was especially rough. His foul mouth on hers made her ill just thinking about it. Then there was Jennifer, the raging lesbian. She was very aware that Liz couldn't get into that scene and it was starting to annoy her. Eddie, on the other hand, didn't have a clue. He just did his thing.

Her options were very limited at this point. She could play along with them. Act like she loved it. Rule that one out. She could try to pit one against the other. Again, that would involve becoming sexually responsive, something she was not prepared to do.

The situation had to get more positive. The dark smelly room was not conducive to sanity. Clothes would help. The panty wardrobe was getting old. Maybe they would agree to let her have some reading material, like a Bible. "A little sunshine and exercise would certainly be nice," she mused.

She was brought up as a Baptist, but like so many people she let other things take precedent. She had a keen sense of her spiritual need in this hellhole. She hated it took something like this to get her tuned in spiritually.

Liz decided she needed to start talking. What did she have to lose?

~

Fishing was slow on the pier. Jake couldn't stop thinking about this mess with Liz. With everyday that passed, hope was fading. It was odd that no ransom demand had surfaced. That was not good news. A sudden tug on Jake's line startled him. He missed the fish and lost his bait.

The feeling was that it had to be an outsider. Jake was not so sure. The strange events of the previous year were relayed to the FBI. They obviously had not taken any of them seriously. They figured it was either a coincidence or a neighborhood juvenile. Either way, in their collective minds it did not add up to abducting the richest woman in South Carolina. At least that was the Fed's reasoning. Everybody was leaning toward the ransom theory.

A sharp tug on the line produced a nice spot for Jake. "I'll think later," he said to himself, "it's time to fish now."

~

"Eddie Britain," FBI agent Homer Southard said as he looked across the desk at Eddie. "I see you got into a little trouble a few years back. Troubling childhood, huh?"

Eddie did not respond.

"Says here that you slapped a female classmate. Got you suspended for thirty days." He looked over his glasses and said, "You got something against girls, Eddie?"

"She called me a stupid redneck. She said it in front of my friends. I was embarrassed."

"You got a girlfriend, Eddie?"

"Yes sir."

"She around here?"

"I live with her."

Southard looked intently at Eddie while tapping his finger on the desk. "That Liz Swanson, pretty good-looking woman wouldn't you say, Eddie?"

Eddie didn't respond right away. This jerk was getting on his nerves. He had to keep cool. "Anybody who isn't blind can see that," he said.

"Did you make her acquaintance, Eddie?"

"I saw her, I knew who she was. I never met her," Eddie said coldly.

"You ever fantasize about her, Eddie. Getting nasty with her?"

Eddie smiled a sinister smile. "I think about stuff like that all the time if that's what you mean. Young people do a lot of that in case you've forgotten."

"You think you're real smart, don't you?" Homer said closing the file. "Don't leave town. That would make us real suspicious," he said in a condescending tone.

"I work everyday. I ain't goin' nowhere. I'm at your beck and call," he said as he walked out.

Homer scratched Eddie off the list. "Much too stupid," he said to himself. "Next," he yelled out the door as Shirley walked in. "This is more like it," he thought as Shirley waltzed in and closed the door.

"At your service," she said. Homer had to smile.

CHAPTER 11

The letter was addressed, Swanson, Chesterfield, Myrtle Beach, SC. It was mailed from Charleston. FBI Agent Southard and Sergeant Rogers watched as Jerry Swanson opened it up. It read:

> We've got your girl
> She is alive
> We want money
> Do you want to play?
> Respond in personals
> Columbia paper this Friday

"Let the games begin," Homer said.

Rudy nodded in agreement. Finally something to go on.

Jerry hung his head and said softly, "She's alive," as tears welled up in his eyes. He was willing to pay any amount to get her back even if it meant bulling his way through the police and the FBI. She was coming home.

"It could be a fake. The woods are full of crackpots," Rudy said. "They're gonna have to show us something."

"What are we going to do?" Jerry asked.

"We're gonna play," Homer returned.

"I don't know what your policies are. This is my wife we're talking about. If they want money, they get money. I just want her back."

"I understand your concern. Everybody wants her back and back safely. We just have to take things a step at a time," Homer said. "These things are unpredictable. The only thing that is certain is that we are dealing with a dangerous element. They cannot be trusted to do what they say. We have to first determine whether or not this is legit. They've got to give us some proof that they have your wife and that she is unharmed. When they deliver that much, then we go from there. The longer we play their game, the better chance we have of them messing up and tipping their hand."

"If they know that we're on to them Liz will be in greater danger. I cannot accept that."

"She's in danger now, Mr. Swanson," Homer said.

Jerry went to the window and gazed at the street. He was a man who had spent his life being in control. His storybook life was in shambles. "Bring her home," he softly said.

~

The rain started to fall in mid-afternoon. Within minutes it was pouring with the strength found only in a coastal storm. The rain pummeled the little building cooling things down. She hoped it would last all night. Maybe it would keep her tormentors away. It did. She thanked God for the rain.

~

In the "I Saw You" section of the Friday Columbia paper the ad simply read: "I want to play. How do I know it's you? You name the terms."

Jerry Swanson sat on the back deck and looked at the ad. The phones in the house were connected to tracing devices. The house was full of policemen. Linda was busy doing her work and wishing this thing would get over with.

Homer Southard took a seat next to Jerry. This kind of luxury was something he'd never know on his FBI pension. Homer led a simple life, too simple for those who knew him. His idea of splurging was treating his wife to a milkshake.

Jerry did not particularly like Homer but he was trying to be gracious just because it was the right thing to do. "Wait and see," Jerry said half to himself.

Homer picked up the sports page, muttered something to himself and said, "You never know about these clowns. I can't imagine them being stupid enough to call here. Like I said, you never know."

They figured it would take a week to get a response. That is, unless they called. They could call from a pay phone without detection if they took less than two minutes.

The numbers were not encouraging when it came to ransoms following abductions. Less than thirty percent of the hostages were released upon the payment. Five percent were released safe without payment. Eighty percent suffered emotional or physical abuse. Eighty-five percent of females were sexually assaulted.

Swanson did not need to hear this stuff now. Retirement was looking better every day for Homer Southard. He had more interrogation of Shirley planned for tonight, "Somebody has to do it," he said to himself with a smile.

What had been a week seemed like a year. Liz lay on the bed and gazed at the dim light from the ceiling. It was getting toward evening. They'd be coming in a couple hours. Living in this hellhole was taking its toll on her health. Under the best of circumstances Liz only weighed 115 pounds. She had already lost ten pounds and half her strength. The stench was terrible. Jennifer at least had the courtesy to bring clean sheets every few days, no doubt for her own well being. At times a fever would come over Liz. Not a big rise, but enough to cause a sweat on her brow.

She counted blocks on the wall for everyday that went by. How much longer could this thing last? Had her captives tried to contact anyone? What was Jerry doing? How was he holding up? Would she ever be able to tell him all that she had endured?

The evening light told Liz they would be coming soon. She heard the dogs reacting. She hoped they were getting tired of her. No such luck.

After two hours of perversion, they were ready to leave.

"You're good, baby. We'll be back tomorrow," Eddie said as he headed out.

"Wait," Liz said. She was terrified. "I need to talk," she managed.

Eddie smiled his evil smile as he looked at Jennifer, "She wants to bond with us. How nice. Does that mean you're gonna start kissing me?" he said as he brought his lips toward hers. She turned away.

"Oh, I see. You want to talk to me but you're too good to kiss me. Bitch!"

"Leave her alone, Eddie," Jennifer said. Jennifer sat on the edge of the bed as Eddie got up. "What is it?" she said.

Liz gasped as she tried to catch her breath. "I'll give you money. I'll have it delivered anywhere you want. Please, I can't take much more of this."

"Just how you gonna do that?" Eddie asked. "Drive to the bank and say 'give me some cash, I'm being abducted?'"

"I can arrange it. There are creative ways," Liz said.

"Look darling, I know we're gonna get some money from your sweet ass. I just ain't in no hurry," he said as he rubbed her leg. "I might just keep you here for years. Wouldn't that be nice? I tell you what we do need though. We need some information. You see we've been in touch with your significant other. He thinks we might just be pulling his chain." Liz's heart raced as he talked. Eddie continued, "Tell me something that I can pass on that will prove to your old man that we've got you and you are still alive. If you wanna ever go free, this better be good."

She thought for a moment, "New Zealand," she said.

"New Zealand?" Eddie questioned.

"Yes, its been our dream. We've always wanted to visit there. He will know it's me."

"You did good, baby. This calls for a celebration," he said as he forced his lips toward hers.

"Get off me you stinking pig!" she spat.

The force of Eddie's slap knocked Liz against the wall. Her lip was bleeding as her cold eyes bore into him.

"Get in the house!" Jennifer ordered. "I mean it Eddie, get out of here!"

He kicked the door open as he stomped out.

Jennifer sat in the chair and lit a cigarette.

"No thanks," Liz said as Jennifer offered her one.

"Well . . . talk to me," Jennifer said. "The jerk has left, in case you haven't noticed."

Liz took a deep breath, "I'm not an animal and I don't like being treated like one. Maybe I will have a cigarette," she said as Jennifer handed her one.

She took a long drag. "I would appreciate some clothes to wear and something to read, novels and a Bible." She hesitated to check for a reaction. She did not get one.

Liz continued, "This place is not healthy. I've been feverish the last couple of days. I wish there was some way I could get some fresh air and a chance for a little exercise."

Jennifer smiled, "How about breakfast in bed? I might be able to arrange for some Latin guy to come in here and give you a massage. Anything else you can think of?" She drew a couple more long drags. "This ain't Chesterfield. The air here is as fresh as it's gonna get."

"I meant what I said about the money. I can come up with whatever you want."

"Yeah, and I bet when you go free you're not gonna put the finger on us either, are you?"

"With some clear thinking and plenty of resources, I would think that you could get lost, maybe change your identity. A fresh start and the money to make it happen."

"I tell you what, when you figure out just how we could pull this thing off and everybody live happily ever after, you let me know," Jennifer said. She studied Liz closely. "You don't care for my loving much do you?"

Liz did not answer which was an answer in itself.

"You just can't get into it, what a shame. We could have had such a good time." She put out her cigarette and got up. "Eddie now, he don't much care what you think or feel does he? That's his style." She started to leave, "Take these," she said handing Liz a small bottle of aspirin. She left without saying anything else.

◈

The dog's loud barking rudely awakened Jake. It was not the bark indicating a cat or another dog, it was definitely a person coming to the door. Sure enough the door bell rang. "Just a minute," he yelled as he pulled on his pants. Looking through the blinds he saw that it was Sally.

"Good boy, Amos," she said as she walked in. "You forgot didn't you?"

"Forgot what?" he thought as he tried to shake the cobwebs out of his head. He was awake enough to notice how nice Sally's legs looked in the Bermudas she was wearing.

"Wilmington," she said with a "you got to know what I'm talking about" look. "Have you been drinking a lot of diet cokes?"

"I can't remember. Want some bacon and eggs?"

"I don't eat that stuff. Grapefruit and bran for me."

"Boring," Jake thought. He started frying his bacon when he realized that today they were going to Wilmington to rendezvous with her sister. "What time are we supposed to meet her?" he said as if he had known it all along. "Kate, I think that's her sister's name," Jake thought.

"The last thing I said to you last night was 1:15 in Wilmington. We meet Shelly at 1:15. Does Alzheimer's run in your family?"

"I can't remember."

"Your girl's in the paper again," she said as she handed him the front page.

The headline read, "Tension Mounts as Jerry Swanson Waits." The article covered several columns and was complete with a picture of Jerry and Liz Swanson. Homer Southard and Rudy Rogers were heading up the law enforcement efforts. The article expressed frustration over the lack of progress. Not a day passed without something about it in the news. It was the main coffee break topic from Virginia Beach to Savannah.

It turned out to be a nice day for a ride. Jake and Sally always enjoyed their little outings. It was the kind of outing married people would enjoy. This was about as close to acting married as either one of them were interested in.

Sally put her favorite country CD into the car stereo and pulled the tab on a cold beer.

"What are the prospects of that girl coming home alive?" she asked as if Jake knew. "I tell you the truth, I would be very surprised if anyone ever sees her alive again," she went on. "I'd hate to think what she has been through."

"Evidently they want money," Jake said.

"How much you think they'll ask for? She comes from serious money, and that Jerry Swanson isn't exactly worried where his next meal is coming from either. I'm sure they'll want more than a million."

"They might need an agent," Jake said. "Are you looking for a job?"

Sally shook her head and said, "No wonder your first wife is dead. She couldn't take any more of you."

"That's a fact. I was more than the poor girl could handle," Jake said as seriously as he could.

Sally sipped her beer and smiled. "I wouldn't know," she said as they tore up the highway.

They met Shelly at a trendy waterfront restaurant. She was great fun and knew every bad joke ever uttered. It was apparent that Sally had the looks in the family. The girls did some shopping in the waterfront area and Jake fed birds and people-watched while waiting on a bench overlooking the shipyard. All in all it was a great day. It was dark when Sally let Jake out at his house with a kiss and a wink.

Jake needed a day of good company and bad jokes. He slept well that night.

CHAPTER 12

The note came in the Thursday mail. It read:

> We're so glad you want to play.
> We want five million dollars.
> Don't you just love New Zealand?
> We will be in touch.
> Be sure to check your mail.

Sergeant Rogers studied the note. There was no doubt now. They did have the girl. No new information could be found from the note. It was typed from the same typewriter as the previous one. This letter was postmarked in Wilmington, the one before in Charleston. There was no way to track the letter's origin.

The area postmasters were alerted to be on the lookout for any personal mail coming to Jerry Swanson. They would have to be extremely lucky to stumble onto anything. The police would like to consider their trade a science, and it certainly was, but many crimes would go unsolved without an element of luck. Rudy was hoping for a little luck on this one.

Jerry and Homer were having a heated argument on the back deck.

"I don't care what your policies are. This is Myrtle Beach, Liz is my wife, and I am paying what they want!" Jerry shouted.

"I can understand your situation, Mr. Swanson, but there are ways that this must be handled."

"She's my wife. I call the shots. Do you understand me?"

FBI agent Southard downed his coffee and looked at Jerry, "Whatever you say, boss. It's your money and your wife. I'm just saying you could be making a big mistake."

Life for Liz was thankfully a little less eventful. Eddie had not been back to harass her since he had slapped her. Jennifer came in nightly with food, towels and some basic hygiene supplies. She did not provide clothes. Eddie wouldn't allow it. He said it would make escape easier. She did provide Liz with a Bible and a couple of novels.

The only fresh air she got was when Jennifer came. She would leave the door opened while she was there. Since the abuse had stopped Jennifer usually did not spend more than fifteen minutes. She had little to say when she came in. She did say the ransom business was coming along.

The chance of overpowering Jennifer and escaping was slim. Jennifer was bigger and thirty years younger. Not to mention that four weeks in this hole without exercise had taken a toll on Liz's strength. Even if she could get by Jennifer, she shuddered to think how she would get by the dogs. They were vicious and huge.

As the days went by Liz found herself reading the Bible and praying. She had always considered herself to be a Christian. Like so many people she had put her faith on the back burner. She regretted her previous spiritual neglect but now felt completely at one with her Creator. It gave her a peace that could not be understood by intellect or reason. Though she was weak, she was strong.

He pulled into Eddie's drive. It was about noon. Eddie was at work, and Jennifer was sprawled out on the couch. A tap on the door woke her from her half sleep. She saw him but he did not see her. He was a tall young man, probably thirty or so and was about a week late on a shave. He was handsome and looked a little wild. Visitors were far and few between. This was one visitor that Jennifer was pleased to see.

"Yes," she said as she cracked open the door.

"Eddie here?"

"Who wants to know?"

"Sidney Lawton, ma'am, friend of Eddie's from Georgetown, and you?"

"The name is Jennifer. How did you know Eddie from Georgetown? He never told me about a Sidney."

"We worked together at Alton Mill. His old girlfriend was named Amber. He lived in Georgetown for about five years. He's got a cousin that lives there. He drinks beer and likes acid rock. How am I doing?"

She wasn't sure about inviting the guy in. He obviously was an old friend of Eddie's. What the heck she thought as she opened the door. "Would you care for a beer?" she said.

"Thanks," he said as he sat down. He had to admire her figure as she got them a couple beers out of the fridge. She handed him a beer and started to undress.

Eddie got home about 6:30. Jennifer and Sidney were relaxing in the living room, sitting in opposite chairs and fully clothed.

"Sidney, you dog," Eddie grinned as Sidney tipped his beer.

"Just enjoying some hospitality. You got a good girl here."

"She has her moments. She can be very social," Eddie added. Jennifer and Sidney just smiled.

"He ain't seen nothing yet," Jennifer thought.

"What brings you up this way?" Eddie asked.

"Came to collect that money you owe me," he joked. "Just came to see my good buddy. Since when do I need an excuse for that?"

"How's everything in Georgetown?" Eddie asked.

"About the same. Same old dead place. The mill is still a sweat shop. Blacks are getting more uppity every day, same old junk. Mary left me about a month ago. Glad to get rid of that loser. You could say I'm in limbo."

"Doing without for a while might do you some good," Eddie said.

"Right," Sidney said. "I've already been doing without about thirty minutes," he thought.

He was in no hurry to leave. That was for sure. The prospect of spending all day alone with Jennifer for a few weeks was not the worst thought he ever had.

"So you on vacation or what?"

"Kind of. Had a little bit of a disagreement with Brandon. You remember that jerk? I got tired of his bull. That supervisor crap just went to his head.

He got to be power hungry. Started kissing up to management. I just told him where to get off," Sidney said as he popped another beer.

Eddie remembered Sidney's habit of drinking everybody else's beer. "So did they fire you?"

"They gave me what they called an 'extended leave of absence.' They said they would re-evaluate the situation later. I've been at that sweat shop too long. I wouldn't go back if they wanted me, which I don't think they do."

"So what you gonna do?"

"You ask a lot of questions. Tonight I'm gonna drink a few beers and party. I ain't worrying about it tonight."

And worry they didn't. Eddie and Sidney got loaded. They drank all the beer in the house and then sent Jennifer on a run for more. When she went out for beer, she stopped back at the dog lot to do whatever she needed to do for Liz. Sidney did not notice.

Several days went by with Eddie going to work, leaving Sidney and Jennifer alone to entertain each other. They had no trouble finding things to do. On a couple of occasions Sidney walked back to the dog lot. He had zero interest in getting inside the fence with those dogs. They did not like him at all. Smart dogs.

"Have I met this guy?" Sally asked as they got into the car.

"I don't think so. I've thought too much of you to introduce you," he smiled. "To say he's a little crusty would be an understatement. He does have a sweet wife, however. You will like her."

"Okay," she said with eyebrows raised as they drove on in silence.

"My God Jake, you said she was ugly," Joe Lane said to Jake when he opened the door. "She's even good looking by my high standards."

"Sally, this is Joe Lane."

"The pleasure is mine," Sally said.

"Hello Jake," Jane Lane said as she came into the hall from the kitchen. "This must be Sally? So glad to have you in our home, dear," she said warmly extending her hand.

The girls hit it off immediately as they headed off talking about curtains, bath towels, and other such interesting subjects.

"Hey, what you say we switch girls tonight? You been holding out on me, boy," Joe said with his big stupid grin.

"Jane needs to kick your stinking ass. She really does. What that good woman sees in you will forever be a mystery to me."

"I tell you what, cowboy, I'm packing some stuff that only a woman could appreciate. Know what I mean?" he winked.

"I know you're getting senile. That I know."

Jane prepared a great meal of barbecued chicken, spinach casserole, Caesar Salad, and stuffed baked potato. As if they needed anything else, she topped it off with strawberry shortcake. "It's a wonder Joe doesn't weigh four hundred pounds," Jake thought.

"Heard anything new about that mess with the Swanson girl?" Jane asked.

"No, I sure haven't," Jake said. "Could you pass me that casserole Jane? This great cooking must be why Joe has such a boyish figure," Jake chuckled.

"Looks like you haven't missed any meals either," Joe said.

Jake had certainly heard enough of Joe's insults to not let them ruin a good meal. "Everybody seems to think that this is a cut and dry ransom case," Jake said to Jane. "It just seems strange to me that they are so slow moving. If I were holding someone like her for ransom, I believe I would get the ball rolling. This crowd seems to be taking their sweet time. To me that just doesn't make sense."

"It all seems so scary to me. From what I've read, she seems like a really decent person," Jane said. "It gives me the creeps."

"Must be an outside job," Joe said. "I mean, how could somebody hit the family up for a pile of money and know them? That would be like, oh yeah, here's your money, and by the way, arrest Bob."

"I just hope the poor girl's alive," Sally said.

~

At 8:25 Thursday morning Rudy Rogers got the call. It was from the postmaster of the Myrtle Beach Post Office. A suspicious letter for Jerry

Swanson had arrived in the morning mail. Rudy grabbed his coffee and headed out the door.

Rudy picked up the letter and headed for Chesterfield. When he arrived Jerry and Homer were waiting. Jerry opened the letter. It read:

> Your girl is fine. She hopes for your cooperation. We want the money in a briefcase under the booth next to the mural on the immediate left at the Oyster Bar Restaurant on 16th. Jerry Swanson is to make the delivery drop at 1:30 p.m. on August Fourth. The pick-up person will be wearing a red ball cap. If any of this gets leaked the girl is dead. If the pick-up person is apprehended or followed, the girl is dead. She means nothing to us. We will kill her if you doublecross us. Do we have a deal? Respond in the Columbia paper.

"We have two weeks. I wonder why they're buying time?" Homer thought out loud. "Why not get it over with?"

"Maybe they're bluffing," Rudy said. "They might try to up the stakes."

"How do we know they'll let her go?" Jerry asked.

"We don't," Homer answered.

"If we try holding out, they might kill Liz. We can't take that chance. We have to give them the money and hope they let her go," Jerry said.

"If they show, we will have a tail. We just have to be creative. We will not put your wife in any additional danger, Mr. Swanson. You can be sure of that. Bottom line is we cannot afford to take these people at their word."

The next day the Columbia paper had the simple phrase in the Personals: "We have a deal."

CHAPTER 13

By this time Liz had been in captivity two full months. It seemed like a hundred years. No human kindness, very little light of day, basically no clothing, terrible abuse, and unclean conditions were starting to wear her down. For the past several weeks she had done situps and pushups to try to stay strong. The few novels she had to read and the Bible gave her what little bit of joy she could muster up. For the most part, the daily sexual abuse had stopped. Occasionally, Eddie would stumble down to the lot in a drunken state and force himself upon her. Lately, those assaults were becoming less and less frequent. Liz attributed it to prayer.

Out of the blue one day Jennifer brought Liz some clothes. They included underwear, shoes, socks, some jeans and a blouse. Liz could wear some of Jennifer's stuff, though by now it was quite baggy. Liz's weight had dipped below a hundred pounds. Jennifer brought her a change of clothes everyday and picked up the dirty ones.

Just the simple concept of having clothes to wear gave Liz both hope and dignity. For the first time in weeks Liz began to think that maybe she was going to survive this ordeal. She continued to pray.

A week before the pick up, Eddie, Sidney and Jennifer were in the trailer drinking beer on a hot summer evening. Eddie had decided that Sidney could be of help. Up to this point Sidney knew nothing about the girl in the dog lot. Tonight that was going to change.

"Wouldn't it be nice to have some serious money?" Eddie asked Sidney. "I mean serious money, like several million?"

"Now that would be nice. The only way anyone ends up with money is by inheriting it. All this junk about self-made millionaires is a bunch of crap. You gotta have money to make it. I guess a couple of slugs like us have to just keep on dreaming."

Eddie sipped his beer and spoke. "I have a plan going that could be the biggest thing in town." He studied Sidney for a response. There was none. "Yes sir, I got our meal ticket within shouting distance of here."

"What you going to do? Start selling snake meat?" Sidney said.

"I wonder if you've got big-time balls or are you just a nickel-and-dime punk?" Eddie asked him.

"I got enough balls to handle anything around here. That's for damn sure."

Jennifer had to agree with that. She listened carefully to the dialogue but did not enter in.

"You think a million dollars is worth chancing jail for, Sidney? Like I said, or are you nickel-and-dime at heart?"

"I'm game, Eddie. What's your point?"

Eddie stood up and waved for Sidney to follow him out the door. Jennifer was close behind.

Liz heard the dogs barking and some voices. She thought she heard a different male voice. The door flew open and the three of them walked in.

"Sidney, meet Liz Swanson."

Sidney stood there with his mouth open for several moments. "Oh hell!" was all he could finally manage.

Back at the trailer Sidney drank several more beers. Eddie and Jennifer described the events of the past few months, including the ransom and the upcoming pick up. Eddie wanted Sidney to do the pick up. Sidney was all smiles. Lady luck was finally turning his way.

Rudy's peculiar behavior told Jake that something was going on with the Liz Swanson deal. There were some things that he was not going to be told. Something was in the air concerning the ransom.

After a quick stop for a biscuit Jake would head off to Georgetown. Things were slow this late July morning at the Beach Deli. Jill brought Jake his coffee and biscuit and sat down with him.

"Thanks Jill," Jake said. "Where's all your boy friends this morning?"

"I hope my boyfriend is calling his broker and making his million dollar deal," she said. Jake noticed the lines around Jill's eyes. Father Time was even talking his toll on her.

"I'm sure there's a prince out there somewhere. Probably just around the corner," Jake said.

"Not sitting across from me?" she winked.

"I'm too old for you and we both know it. Besides I got a weak heart."

Jill cupped her coffee and looked out the window. "Most of the guys I know are so immature. They don't care about tomorrow. All they want is a new trophy. I'm getting a little old for that game," she said. "And no, you're not that old. You're not quite as old as dirt, close, but not quite. Anything new on the Swanson lady?"

"Not that I know of. Rudy's not telling me the whole deal. Something's around the corner. I just don't know what. I'm going down to Georgetown today to do a little snooping around. I really don't expect to find anything. What are you doing the rest of the day?" Jake asked hopefully.

Jill embraced Jake's forearm and laid her head on his shoulder. "I just need a pal, Jake. I don't need a daddy or a man. I just need a pal. Is that okay?"

Jake stroked her hair and said, "That's great. A pal is excellent." This pretty, young girl didn't want to hurt his feelings. He was touched.

"I'm gonna have to stay around here. It will get busy soon. You have a good time and stay clear of those wild Georgetown widows. I've heard about some of them," she said as she got up to wait on a couple that had just come in.

"My new pal has a great butt," Jake noticed as she walked away. Jake finished his coffee and headed for Georgetown.

He arrived in Georgetown at 10 in the morning. Not knowing what else to do, he went to see Millie Stackpole on Cedar Street. The wind was blowing toward the southwest and the stench from the paper mill was heavy. The folks living in the area didn't seem to mind. It was just like every other day in this part of Georgetown. With the address in hand and a vague recollection, Jake found her house.

When he arrived, Millie's son Skoo was working on an old Ford truck. He looked at Jake with cold eyes. A trace of recognition came across his face. "Guess you lookin' for Mamma?" he said.

"I sure am. Skoo, wasn't it?" Jake asked.

"Dat's right."

"What's wrong with the truck?"

"Won't start. Think it's the fuel filter. Got some water in it. Been sittin' too long."

Jake nodded his head as if he fully understood. Skoo obviously was an intelligent young man. Like so many young blacks he had ten strikes against him most of his life. Jake handed Skoo a rag and a wrench as he took off the fuel filter. "I can give you a ride to get that replaced," Jake offered.

"Dat would be nice. Let me tell Mamma we're goin'."

A few minutes later they headed to the local parts store. Skoo didn't say anything to Jake but he wasn't hostile either. Progress was being made. Back at the house, he replaced the filter and the truck cranked up. Jake was impressed.

"I guess you've heard about Mrs. Swanson being abducted up at the Beach?" Jake asked Skoo.

"Have to be from the moon to not hear 'bout dat."

"Sorry, I didn't mean it like that," Jake said trying not to put the young man on the defensive. "It's just that we're not making much progress. Have you heard anything that could be a help? We just want to get to the bottom of this."

"Ain't heard nothin'. She's a good lady. Not uppity. Ain't heard nothin'."

They walked to the porch just as Millie Stackpole came out. Skoo nodded to Jake as he went inside and left them on the porch.

"Smart young man," Jake said.

Millie shook her head in agreement and said, "Never stop worryin 'bout yo' chilin." She sat down in the rocking chair, lit up her cigarette and took three or four long drags.

"We're not making any progress concerning Mrs. Swanson. I just didn't know what to do so I came down here to check around. Have you heard anything at all?"

She just shook her head a sad no. "I be surprised if she still alive," she said. "It's a cruel world," she said staring into the street as the wind chimes sounded from the end of the porch.

"I wanted to give you my card in case you need to call me about anything. Call collect anytime day or night."

"Thanks. I believe you gave me one, but thanks." She took the card and laid it on the porch rail. "Care for some tea?"

"I believe I would."

They drank tea and rocked in the summer breeze on the front porch for an hour or so before Jake thanked her for her time and headed back to Myrtle Beach.

≈

Calvary Temple was rocking this summer Sunday morning. Maintenance man, Jerome Haze, his wife Donna, and their small children, Herbie and Sarah, were regular fixtures in this Pentecostal church. The Swanson's maid, Linda, was definitely feeling the Spirit.

"Lord. Praise the Lord. Hallelujah, thank you Jesus," Linda praised as they were leaving church. "I just wanna shout. Dear God, this is great."

"I'll be glad when you get excited girl," Donna Haze said. "Don't know what I'd do without my sweet Lord."

"Speaking of sweet, I'll bet that sweet potato pie is gonna hit the spot. Linda girl, you're gonna enjoy my sweet Donna's wonderful cookin'," Jerome said.

"I tell you what, Donna, he is bragging on you every time I see him," Linda said.

Donna put her hands on her hips, tilted to her side and said to Linda, "If he knows what's good for him, he better be braggin on me."

They finished the main meal then enjoyed coffee and pie. Linda started to get up to clear the dishes.

"You just sit down. You are not a maid in this house. You are our guest. These dishes can wait. Jerome can do them later," she smiled.

Donna began to massage Linda's neck. "I sure hope this thing breaks soon. I know its terrible hard on you, girl," Donna said.

"It's worse than a nightmare. I can't wake up from this one. They're hoping some progress is on the way, I'm not sure what. The FBI doesn't talk to the domestic help," Linda said.

Jerome poured coffee all around. "I know they figure it's an outside job. I'm not so sure."

"What you mean, baby?" Donna asked.

"My co-worker has been acting strange since this whole thing came down."

"You must mean Eddie?" Donna said. "He's a strange dude anyway."

"One in the same. I just can't put my finger on it. He would be the first one to run his mouth about this kind of thing. But the guy never brings it up. He has a thing against rich people. He loves to see them in trouble and he ain't saying nothing. Completely out of character for him."

"Have you said anything to anyone?" Linda asked.

"I said something to Lenny. He didn't have much to say. He said there was no way Eddie would be smart enough to pull this off. He just shrugged it off. I tend to agree. Eddie's no Einstein. He's just acting weird, very weird."

Linda kept what Jerome said in mind. Tomorrow she was going to talk to someone.

⁓

The tension showing in the faces of those at the Swanson house told the story. It was two days before the delivery and there was nothing to do but wait. Jerry Swanson spent part of the morning talking to Republican officials in the state legislature. The rest of the time he was talking to family members on the phone. Sergeant Rogers was busy with the surveillance logistics surrounding the Oyster Bar Restaurant.

Two plants were already in place, one as a hostess, the other as a waiter. The hostess, Shannon Hairrston, was a detective with the Myrtle Beach Police Department with five years experience in undercover vice work. She often posed as a prostitute in an effort to curb the city's problem in this area. She was a qualified "sharpshooter" and had a third degree black belt in karate. The waiter, Leon Jones, was a three-year detective and former linebacker for the University of North Carolina. He could handle about any situation. They were both very bright and professional. They represented the best Myrtle Beach had to offer. Rudy felt good about their chances.

Homer Southard had several of his men planted in locations on all sides of the Oyster Bar Restaurant. Arrangements had been made with the local air station concerning helicopter surveillance once the pick up was made.

The money had been withdrawn and was in the vault at the Swanson residence. The five million gave the Swanson net worth quite a jolt, but they were certainly not going to be left destitute. Jerry wanted Liz back home no matter what the cost.

"Care for coffee?" Linda asked Sergeant Rogers.

Rudy rubbed his head and chuckled. "I guess I look like I need it. Thanks Linda."

The Swanson's were extremely classy people and their choice of Linda as their domestic help certainly reflected it.

Linda joined Rudy for a cup of coffee. "Good time to catch up on your praying," she said with a smile.

Rudy smiled, "Yeah, I've fallen a little behind in that area. You might get me to change my ways though."

"I can't do that but I bet God could."

Rudy just shook his head in agreement.

"So, we should know something in a couple days?" Linda asked.

"Hopefully."

Linda straightened her skirt and starred out the window. "I had lunch with some friends yesterday, Jerome Haze and his wife Donna. They are really great people. You've probably seen Jerome. He's a maintenance man here in the development." Rudy nodded his head that he knew him. "Anyway," she continued, "he told me that his co-worker, Eddie, has been acting strange."

"How's that?" Rudy asked.

"Jerome said that ever since this thing with Mrs. Swanson came down, that Eddie has been acting strange. He said that Eddie hardly ever talks about it. To Jerome, that's what seemed so strange. Eddie is the kind of guy who would really get off on this kind of thing. He loves to see rich people brought down. He loves running his mouth about every little thing, but this, this has been different. I don't know. It's probably nothing. I just felt like I needed to say something to you."

Rudy took in all that she said. "I appreciate the information. I've talked to Jerome and Eddie. Eddie did seem like a strange bird. There was something about him that I didn't much care for. I guess at the time I just didn't see him as the kind of mastermind that could pull this kind of thing off. I do appreciate the information and I will keep it in mind."

"I just want her home. That's all I want," Linda said as she wiped a tear from her eye.

"I know. That's what we all want."

CHAPTER 14

The fourth of August was a typical hot South Carolina day. The sky was clear and the streets were packed with little kids eating ice cream and college girls in skimpy bathing suits being followed by droves of teenage boys.

The Oyster Bar Restaurant had finished a busy breakfast and was gearing up for the lunch crowd. A Greek family had owned it for thirty years. They had made their million several times over. By the looks of business, there was much more to be made.

They were assured that there would be no violence. The drop off and pick up should go unnoticed by their customers. Shannon Hairrston and Leon Jones were the in-store contacts. Shannon, as the hostess, would insure that the correct table was unoccupied and Leon would be the waiter.

Greek Salads and cheese steak sandwiches were the big movers during lunch. The crowd started thinning out before one. Five minutes before the scheduled drop at one twenty-five, there were seven customers in the restaurant.

At precisely one twenty-five, Jerry Swanson pulled into the parking lot. His job was simple. He was to walk in the door and be escorted to the table under the mural by Shannon Hairrston. Once seated he was to order a Danish and coffee. After his food came, he was to leave the moneybag under the table. He was not to be familiar in any way with either the hostess or the waitress. At two o'clock he was to leave, get in his car and drive home. The police would keep him informed as things developed.

"A table for one?" Shannon asked when Jerry walked into the restaurant.

"Yes, just one."

"This way please," she said as she led him to the correct table.

Jerry did his best to remain calm. If the truth were known, he had never been so nervous in all his life. He took the seat facing away from the front door.

"My name is Elliot. I will be your server. Could I get you something to drink?" Leon Jones asked in a manner that suggested he'd been a waiter before.

"I'll just have a coffee and Danish, please," Jerry said.

"Of course," Leon said as he hurried off to get it.

The coffee and Danish were quickly served. Having something to eat and drink had a surprisingly soothing effect on Jerry's nerves. After three or four sips of his coffee Jerry nonchalantly placed the brief case at his feet near the wall and under the bench he was sitting on.

Leon brought him a refill. Jerry slowly sipped his coffee and studied the other customers. The clientele were definitely tourists. The pick-up guy was not here yet. Jerry found himself uttering a silent prayer with almost every breath he took, "Lord, please keep Liz safe and bring her home."

At exactly 2 he left the restaurant and headed home.

Two couples came in during the next ten minutes. They were placed on the other side of the restaurant.

At 2:20 Sidney Lawton, sporting a red ball cap pulled down toght on his ears, entered the restaurant. He had arrived by cab. He looked around nervously when he walked in.

"That table is not taken is it?" Sidney said to Shannon pointing toward the booth by the mural.

Shannon Hairrston escorted him to the table under the mural and gave him the seat facing away from the door.

"Elliot will be right with you," she said as she walked away.

Not only were Shannon and Leon experts in skills of hand to hand combat, but they were both also highly trained in recognition skills. There would not be much about Sidney's persona that they would miss.

Looking over the menu, Sidney ordered a seafood platter and a coke. His heart raced when he saw the edge of the brief case sticking out from under the bench. Sidney placed his portable phone on the table, turned on and ready to speed dial Eddie's number. He hoped the call would not be needed. If it were made, Liz Swanson would be dead within ten minutes. The phone stayed on the table in full view of any interested parties.

A surveillance camera had been placed less than twenty feet from Sidney. The high-powered lens perfectly captured Sidney's every feature. That, along with the microphone under the table, transmitted signals via phone lines to the FBI's main computer bank in Washington in an effort to identify the pick-up man. Sidney did not realize it quite yet, but his mug would soon be plastered on the wall in every Post Office lobby in America. He was now a known commodity. Sidney, of course, had not thought through the consequences of his actions. All he saw was the money. Somehow cash was going to make everything better in his sad life.

The police plants were stationed around the restaurant. They saw Sidney go in and were positioned to spring into action. There were no police cars near the restaurant and certainly no one in uniform. Everybody was undercover; the officers were inconspicuous, invisible. Playing Russian roulette with Liz's life was not an option.

At 2:50 Sidney called a cab from his table. Five minutes later he picked up the briefcase, paid his bill, walked out of the restaurant, and got into a cab.

Eddie Britain waited by the pay phone on this hot August afternoon in a location seven miles due west from the beach. The call would be the signal to head for the house, go to the shed, kiss Liz good bye, and blow her brains out. That prospect brought a smile to his face as he gripped the pistol in his pocket. The entire process would take about ten minutes. If the call didn't come by 3, Eddie would call Jennifer who would then proceed to the pick-up location to meet Sidney. "Be cool, Sidney," Eddie thought.

"Uptown," Sidney said to the cabby as he got in.

"Whatever you say boss," the driver said. Everything Sidney said was still being transmitted to the Myrtle Beach Police Department via radio waves.

The car was tracked with the use of a sophisticated homing device placed under the front seat of the cab. It transmitted a signal to a computer at police headquarters on Oak Street. The helicopter was staying at a distance and would only be used in case of emergency. Every precaution had to be made concerning Liz Swanson's safety.

Sidney scanned the area. Nothing seemed out of the ordinary. "I need to stop at the store," he said pointing to a gas station. When the car stopped, Sidney slowly got out and peered over the area. "I'll be right back." Inside the station he studied the King's Highway traffic. The cab driver appeared calm but he continually glanced toward the station. The more he observed the driver the more convinced Sidney was that he was a plant. The police had to be trailing him. He bought some mints and got back into the cab.

Sidney spotted several cabs next to the Hilton North. "Stop here," he said. He got out, paid the driver and immediately went to another cab and got in. "Myrtle Place Mall," he said as he glared at the cab driver behind him. "Had to be a cop," he said to himself. "I need let out at the mall food court. I'm in a hurry. How much is it gonna be?"

"Six twenty five," the cabdriver said.

Sidney gave him a twenty, "Keep the change," he said as the cab driver quickly stuck the twenty in his pocket. Still no sign of being tailed. The new driver was unshaven and had disheveled hair. He smelled like he hadn't had a bath in a week. A bandana was wrapped around his head and he was listening to a classic rock station. He was definitely not a cop.

"I need you to help me out a little bit," Sid said to the cabby. "There's a few people following me who don't like me much and I need to ditch them."

"You mean at the mall?" the driver asked.

"That's right. When we get to the mall. I need for you to pull over onto the curb very quickly so the traffic behind us will pass us. A few seconds later I need you to pull into the mall and get me to the food court in a hurry. Can you handle that?"

The cabby, with drool on his lips, grinned a big toothless smile, put on his sunglasses and said, "Rock and Roll!"

Sidney was five minutes from the mall and had a maniac for a cab driver. Once at the mall his plan was simple. Hit the food court fast. Go quickly to the rest room where he would change from his jeans and tank top to slacks and a golf shirt. He would remove the wig he was wearing and apply a mustache. The money would be moved from the briefcase to a shopping bag. This should take no more than two minutes. He would leave the restroom, walk to the food court and meet Jennifer who will be enjoying a slice of pizza. Sidney would then walk by her table. He would stop for a moment, say a couple pleasantries, leave the bag on a chair at the table and walk out the same door he came in. He would get into his waiting car and drive off. Jennifer would be two minutes behind him. If Sidney was apprehended she would keep on walking. If either was apprehended, Liz Swanson was dead.

"Any ideas?" Rudy asked his coordinating team which consisted of several highly skilled people.

"He's feeling us out," John Hampton said. John headed the team up and was a sharp thirty-year old academy grad. "I expect him to make his move soon."

"How many cars are now within sight of him?" Rudy asked.

"Three vehicles. We have a utility truck three cars back. Another cab fifty yards behind the truck. And we have a couple of young officers in a Honda two cars ahead of them."

Rudy shook his head. They couldn't be too careful. Liz's life hung in the balance. There was no room for any grandstand acts today. He had stressed that to his men over and over. Hopefully it sunk in.

Myrtle Place Mall was doing a great Saturday afternoon business. It was filled with a healthy tourist crowd escaping the summer heat. It was also hosting a regional craft show.

Jennifer entered the mall dressed in her finest summer dress with her hair done in the latest yuppie fashion. She was a striking young woman who enjoyed turning all the men's heads. This time it wasn't because of the length of her mini-skirt or the fact she obviously didn't wear a bra. It was just because she was so damn good looking.

Jennifer ordered a slice of pepperoni pizza and a diet coke. She grabbed a seat facing the front door. "Keep cool girl," she told herself. He should be here within five minutes. She was one of hundreds enjoying the food court. "Perfect," she thought.

Jennifer was one of those girls who looked seventeen when she was twelve. As long as she could remember she had been a favorite with the boys. She liked playing the sex card and she was good at it. She could only imagine what her exploits could be if she had some cash. The thought of that prospect had driven her these past several months. She'd dump the clowns she was hanging out with now at her first opportunity. And with her, opportunities were a daily occurrence.

"Stop here," Sidney said as the cab pulled to the curb. Sidney gazed at the cars speeding by on King's Highway. Traffic was heavy and no one could stop even if they wanted to. He watched for twenty seconds. If anyone was following they were passed him by now. "Haul ass!" Sidney yelled.

"Yeeehaaa!" the driver screamed as he sped into the mall parking lot.

The cab pulled up and Sidney jumped out. He was in the door in a flash. The police were still trying to turn around in the heavy traffic. The cab driver sped off from the food court burning rubber, sliding sideways, and screaming something at the top of his lungs.

"What happened?" FBI agent Homer Southard screamed.

"He tripped us up. He's heading for the mall," one of his agents fired back.

"Get in there," Southard screamed.

Sidney's eyes met Jennifer's when he walked in the front door. He went straight to the men's room. One man was using the sink, another the urinal. He went quickly to the handicap stall and closed the door. Forty seconds later he came out of the stall leaving his old clothes in the brief case inside the stall. Checking his mustache in the mirror he grabbed the shopping bag and headed for the food court where Jennifer was waiting. Walking straight to her table he said a quick hello and left the bag on the seat. With a smile and a wink he was on his way.

Sidney was leaving out the front door at the same moment three under cover police agents were coming in the door. He went straight to his car and drove off unnoticed. Jennifer noticed several serious people scanning the food court and motioning to an unseen accomplice. She drew in a breath, sipped the last of her diet coke, picked up the shopping bag filled with five million in unmarked hundred-dollar bills, and headed for the front door.

As serious as the moment was, even the undercover cops took a moment to notice her sensuous sway as she went out the door. She walked to her car, threw the bag onto the back seat, and drove away undetected.

The ass chewing began fifteen minutes later and continued well into the night. Myrtle Beach's finest and the good old boys of the FBI had egg all over their faces. Jerry Swanson spent the evening oscillating between rage and despair. He was very close to the end of his rope. Would he ever see Liz alive again? He was beginning to doubt it.

CHAPTER 15

Jennifer met Eddie at the trailer. He grabbed the shopping bag as Jennifer walked in the door.

"Ain't you some hot stuff?" he said as he sat the money on the table. "How did it go?"

"Too good to be true if you ask me," she said pouring herself some whiskey in a tall glass. "They came in the mall looking for us. The place was packed. They didn't notice Sidney. They passed him in the doorway. The idiots walked right by him. I couldn't believe it. I walked out and nobody noticed. It was perfect. Just plain perfect." The liquor was beginning to calm her nerves.

They walked to the door as Sidney pulled up. He'd already stopped for a bottle on the way home. "Idiot," Eddie thought. Sidney hugged Jennifer and gave Eddie a high five when he walked in.

"Easy street here I come," he said as he took a big gulp of the whiskey he had just bought. "Those clowns didn't pick up on a thing. Like taking candy from a baby."

The party went on for several hours. Before they got too drunk to think, they did agree that the next phase needed to be carefully studied. No need to rush things they all agreed. By 10 p.m. they were passed out for the evening.

∾

The following morning, the mood at the Swanson house on Chesterfield was dismal to say the least. The incomprehensible reality that Liz had not been returned and five million dollars had been kissed away would mess up anybody's day.

Homer Southard was huddled with several FBI agents on the deck. Rudy

Rogers was talking on a cell phone on the front porch with someone downtown, and Jerry Swanson was trying to decide who he was going to strangle first.

Jerry could not for the life of him figure why the so-called experts had not insisted on Liz's imminent return before the money was to be paid. It was explained to him that when dealing with the criminal element those things were worked out as you went. "That's easy to say when you're talking about someone else's wife and money," Jerry angrily thought.

The FBI boys had not been able to come up with a make on the pick-up guy. The unspoken truth around the Swanson house this hot August morning was they were no better off than they were when they first started. In fact they were back to square one and maybe even worse. With every day that passed the prospect of finding Liz Swanson alive was getting slimmer. They've got their money. What would be the point of taking any additional chances by keeping her alive?

A quiet desperation settled in. Hoping against hope they prayed that something would break soon. With their money in hand, maybe now they would let her go.

Sunday morning was like any other day for Liz. Jennifer had not made her daily visit the night before. That in itself was not that terribly unusual. She had no idea of the activities of the previous day. She knew it was Sunday only because she had kept track of the days. It was Sunday, August fifth. She had gotten into the habit of exercising every day. It helped her both physically and emotionally. It had been several weeks since either Eddie or Jennifer had abused her. A fact she was more than a little bit thankful for.

Liz spent a good part of everyday wondering what was going on outside of this dog lot prison. She thought about her dear Jerry. He was such a good man. He had overcome many things in his life. He was always the one who landed on his feet. How was he coping with this? How could anyone cope with this?

Not a hundred yards away in the trailer the hung-over drunks were beginning to stir. With the morning sun came the renewed excitement of the fact that they had apparently gotten away with one of the greatest heists in South Carolina history—pulled off by a group of rank amateurs.

Sidney was sprawled out on the couch thinking about getting up. "Coming up here has worked out real well," he thought. About that time Jennifer walked beside him into the kitchen to make some coffee. Sidney, knowing Eddie was still sleeping, pulled on her panty line as she walked by. She leaned down, gave him a French kiss and pushed him away as she headed for the sink. "It's a wonder Eddie lets you walk around here dressed like that. He's got to know something's up," he said just loud enough for her to hear.

Sidney got up from the couch and sat down at the kitchen table. He could hear Eddie snoring in the other room. He stirred the coffee Jennifer handed him. "Five million split three ways can buy a lot of dreams. I guess you and Eddie got some big plans," he said half mocking. "I'm sure all that money will turn him into a first class human being. Not much doubt about that now is there?"

Jennifer looked at him with a "yeah, right" look. "Who knows what's gonna happen. All I know is the rules have changed," she said as she licked the honey off of her coffee spoon. "This girl has put up with her last loser. This much I know."

She seemed primed to dump Eddie. From the way she had been carrying on with him, Sidney had to feel like he was in good standing. Having some cash and hanging around with Jennifer sounded good. "Maybe we can get Eddie out of the loop. I mean, what are friends for?" Sidney mused.

"We should take the money and get out of town. Leave Mr. Nice Guy behind," Sidney said in not much more than a whisper. "We can go in style, baby, and I mean style."

Jennifer shook her head. "Eddie would track us down and kill us both. You know he would. He just plain doesn't care. I'm afraid of him."

Sidney couldn't argue with that. It was better not to press your luck with Eddie. If they tried to stiff him he would spend his last breath getting even. Eddie would not think twice about killing Sidney.

Jennifer eyed him carefully. "I'm not against considering some things. We just got to be careful that's all."

Sidney smiled as Jennifer got up to start frying the bacon.

The smell of breakfast finally roused Eddie from his drunken stupor. Sitting down at the table he drank a beer instead of coffee with his bacon and eggs.

"I wish you'd drink coffee like a normal person," Jennifer griped.

"I wish you'd shut the hell up," Eddie said as Jennifer got up slamming her plate on the table and storming toward the bedroom. "How about putting some clothes on," he yelled after her.

"I imagine you like seeing her come out here half naked," he said to Sidney.

Sidney gave him a look and kept on eating. Finally Sidney said, "You need to lighten up."

"Oh, I need to lighten up?"

"Yeah, I think you do. We're up to our assholes in unanswered questions in case you haven't noticed. Like what are we gonna to with the broad out back and where are we going to go. We can't just hang around this dump and wait for them to show up."

"If we take off now it's gonna look pretty suspicious at work, don't you think? All of a sudden I'm no longer working there. I mean those people are stupid but I think that even they could figure that one out. We gotta be real careful right now. We can't tip our hand. We will make our move soon. I don't like sitting here anymore than you do. We just got to be smart."

"Smart like getting drunk before noon?" Sidney jabbed.

"Don't push me, Sidney. I mean it. I can be real nasty."

"Whatever," Sidney said as he got up from the table and headed out the door for some fresh air.

❧

"Jake. This is Rudy. What's goin on?"

"Hey Rudy. Not much, I was planning on going out to the pier and fight the coeds for a spot to fish. I'll be out there about five. Come on out. I'll spring for some coffee and I might even give you a fishing tip or two."

"I'll be there," Rudy said as he hung up.

"Been a couple of weeks since I've seen the old boy. Case must be getting him down. It will be good to see him again," Jake thought as he did up his Sunday lunch dishes.

Three hours later he was on the pier.

"Hey dude, how's the fishing?" Rudy asked knowing darn well that the fishing was terrible this time of year.

"You should have seen the whopper I just threw back."

"Right." Rudy leaned on the rail beside Jake and took a long drag on his cigarette. "I need to take up fishing. Golf is going nowhere fast."

"Give yourself some time. You've only been playing what, thirty years? Rome wasn't built in a day you know." Jake sat his pole down and pulled a cold soda from his cooler and took a swig. "I take it things aren't going well with the Swanson case?"

"Not worth a crap." Rudy said putting out his cancer stick on the pier and staring down at a jellyfish slivering near the water's surface. "I thought you might have some words of wisdom for me."

"You mean other than submitting your retirement papers?"

"I mean, I thought maybe you'd have an idea by some ridiculous chance. The Myrtle Beach police and the FBI don't seem to know their ass from a hole in the ground. I'm just getting sick and tired of this whole damn mess."

Jake stared out across the horizon. "I wish I could help you, buddy. I guess you guys are back at square one, huh?"

"Pretty much. We had a ransom pick up yesterday. We had that darn place covered like a glove. The FBI was broadcasting the sucker's mug all over the world. We had tails everywhere, in the restaurant, in the street, in the cab he rode in, and in the air for crying out loud. The clown lost us at the mall of all places. He walked away with a cool five million and not one sign of the girl."

"How did he lose you at the mall?"

Rudy shook his head in disgust. "He must have watched a million B movies. He ducked inside, went to the bathroom, changed his identity, and walked away. We must have walked right by him."

"Were there any surveillance cameras in the mall?"

"There were three cameras in the food court. The place was packed. We are looking at ten or fifteen possibilities. Even if we have a possible make, there are no cameras in the parking lot. He left the mall without a trace."

"I guess you have all point bulletins out with mug shots?"

"We're trying to match up some faces. The department is going to put pictures in the paper. We're working our informant network right now." Rudy brushed his gray hair and said, "The guy's out five million Jake, five damn million. With every second that goes by his wife is in more danger. I'm grasping at straws. I've worked my butt off for thirty years. I've given my best to this outfit. I'm ready to retire, and this thing shows up. I don't need this."

They gazed toward the horizon of the vast Atlantic Ocean. Jake and Rudy cut up a lot. It was one of those man things. They'd been through a lot together. Each understood when the other was hurting. Without saying a word they knew they could count on one another.

After several minutes Rudy said, "You remember Linda? The Swanson maid?"

"Yeah, first class lady."

"For sure. She tells me that she has some concern about one of the maintenance guys, Eddie Britain. He's the tall smart aleck. I've talked to him a couple times. To me the guy's a knucklehead, not near smart enough. Arrogant redneck you might say."

"Happy to say I've not made his acquaintance. What is Linda saying about him?" Jake asked.

"It's not really her, she barely knows the guy. She attends church with his co-worker. Some guy named Jerome. He thinks Eddie has been acting strange about this whole thing."

"How so?" Jake asked.

"By not saying hardly anything about it. I guess that's just not his style. They say he's got a bad attitude toward anyone with a few bucks. This would have been the perfect scenario for him to run his ignorant mouth. Instead, he doesn't bring the subject up."

Jake looked at his friend. "You are grasping at straws. Seems kind of weak, Rudy. Has the guy been showing up for work?"

"Everyday just like always. He's a punk but he shows up."

"Nothing I hate worse than a dedicated punk," Jake said.

Rudy reached into his pocket and handed Jake a piece of paper. "Here's his address. How about figuring out a way to snoop around there. I can't take the chance of cops showing up. If he's our man the girl could get hurt. They wouldn't suspect you."

"What if I get shot or worse?"

"I'll take care of the obituary. Oh, and I'll try to be of some comfort to that girl of yours. Sally isn't it?"

"I could just cry. You're a real pal. You know that?" Jake said.

Rudy smiled.

"Are you sure the Myrtle Beach Police Department can afford me?" Jake asked.

Rudy's smile turned into a laugh. "Between the FBI, the police, and Jerry Swanson, I think we'll manage."

Jake had to smile at that one.

CHAPTER 16

Monday morning Eddie Britain headed off for work. Figuring things out was never one of his strong suits. What was he going to do with Liz? Probably the best thing to do was just kill her. What good was she to him now? With the money he had now he could have all the high society women he wanted.

It didn't take a genius to figure that Jennifer was coming on to Sidney. It was the one thing she could do well. Sidney certainly wouldn't waste five minutes making the move on her. "Yeah, quite a pair," he thought. "Quite a pair."

At this point their little affair did not concern him. What did concern him was them putting their pea brains together and figuring how they could shaft him. Eddie had planted an ace in the hole just in case, an auto-reverse cassette recorder. It was voice activated so it could catch the conversation for most of the day on a ninety-minute tape. Eddie strategically placed it under the kitchen table. Jennifer, being the classy lady that she was, was certainly entertaining the houseguest in her bedroom. Hopefully Eddie wouldn't have to hear that. Eddie was as sick of her as she was of him. They were ready to go their separate ways as soon as the dust settled and they were able to relocate.

As usual Sidney got into bed with Jennifer as soon as Eddie left for work which was about 7:30. They were at the breakfast table by 9.

"We need to make our move. Time is definitely not on our side," Sidney said.

"Where could we go?" Jennifer asked.

"I got a plan. I think you're going to like it."

She gave him that "speak already" look.

"I have a connection in Savannah. Her name is Mary Lou Pratt. She's got connections with the underground and could get us fake IDs. She fixed my cousin up one time. It was totally clean. I tell you the girl does good work. Think about it, totally different people with five million in our pockets."

"What if Eddie finds us?" Jennifer asked.

"How's he gonna do that? Where's he gonna look? Who's he gonna be looking for?"

"He scares me. He always has. He won't rest until he finds us. I know Eddie."

"I've been thinking about that. I got a plan. We leave our boy a note. Tell him we're gone and we've changed our names. If he leaves work to find us we will tip off the police about the little package in the back lot. The cops would be on his tail but quick. He will be forced to stay. If he leaves to come after us, we put the finger on him immediately."

"I don't know, Sid. I can't imagine him taking a shaft job like that lying down. He would be willing to die first," she said.

"Self-preservation is the strongest instinct going. He ain't going to mess with us. Besides, what are we going to do? Wait for him to come up with some nice-guy plan? We need to move and we need to move quick." He hesitated a minute. "I think we should make our move today. It's only a matter of time before things start closing in. It's going to happen. Let's grab the cash and hit the road. We got to do it. The cops don't know we exist. I say we split."

"What about my mom? When will I see her again?"

"It's got to be a clean break. Maybe down the line somewhere you can get in touch. Call her today. Tell her you'll be gone for a while. You will get in touch but it might be a while."

Jennifer was obviously shaken. This thing had spiraled out of control. The last ten years of her life had been a complete mess. She had not done a thing to make her mom proud. Maybe things would be different now. What kind of life could she possibly have hanging around here? She made up her mind right then. She was leaving with Sidney. By noon they were on their way to Savannah but not before one last visit with Liz.

"Here is some stuff you'll need," Jennifer said to Liz as she unlocked the door and walked in.

Liz was surprised to see her this time of day. She always came in the evening. Liz had just finished her exercises and was heavy with perspiration. "I know it's hot in here but you're sweating like a pig," Jennifer said.

Liz wiped her face with a towel and sat down. "I'm just trying to maintain my sanity, a little exercise you know." She noticed the abundant supply of articles that Jennifer had brought with her. "What's the deal with these?" she asked.

"You won't be seeing me again. Eddie's going to be a little hot. I'm not so sure he will be thinking much about your comfort."

"Like you have," Liz thought. "Taking off with Sidney I guess?" she asked.

"Yeah."

"Any chance you could do anything to get me out of here?"

"Look, I'm sorry for everything, okay? I'm sorry Eddie ever brought you here. I'm sorry for the way we treated you. I'm sorry that I don't know what to tell you now." Jennifer took a deep breath and continued. "We got some money from your old man two days ago, five million dollars. We were supposed to let you go. Obviously we didn't. I can't hang around here any longer. When Eddie gets home tonight, I'm gonna be gone. He is going to be furious. I hope he doesn't hurt you. I don't think he will. If he comes after us, we're going to tip off the police. We're leaving you here as leverage so he won't come after us. I am sorry. I'm sure I'll go to my grave being sorry about this."

Liz was in shock. This was the first news she had heard from the outside since she had been here. Her emotions ran from outrage to fear. Outrage at not being released after shelling out five million and fear knowing full well that her life now might not be worth two cents to Eddie. He was a terrifying man. She could only imagine the emotions that Jerry was feeling right now.

"I hope you can find it in your heart to forgive me. I can't see how you could," Jennifer said.

Liz stared at the floor a moment and then looked up at Jennifer. "I can only forgive you because Jesus has forgiven me. That's the best I can do."

Jennifer's eyes became moist and Liz continued, "Would you at least let me write Jerry a short note, just to let him know that I'm all right?"

Jennifer reached into her purse and handed Liz a pad and a pen. Liz wrote:

> Dear Jerry,
> This is Monday, August sixth. I just found out that you paid for my release. This is my first news from the outside of any kind. I want you to know that I am still alive. I pray everyday for my return to you. I can't tell you how much I miss you and love you. My situation has been terrible but I can't help believing that somehow I will be with you again.
> Don't stop believing,
> Love Liz

She handed the note to Jennifer and gave a glancing goodbye.

"Good luck Liz," Jennifer said as she headed out the door. "I'll get this in the mail today." She mailed it somewhere on the way to Savannah.

Eddie arrived at the trailer about 6:30. Pulling into the drive, he noticed Sidney's car was gone. The front door was shut which was quite unusual for August in South Carolina in a house with almost no air conditioning. He unlocked the door and walked in. At his feet was a white envelope. He opened it up, and began to read:

> Eddie,
> All good things must come to an end. You won't be seeing the money or us anymore. We've changed our identities so it won't do any good to try to find us. Don't worry, I'm sure the money will get us through. I know you're thrilled. I'll be checking at Chesterfield to make sure you're still working there. If you decide to quit work and come after us, I guess I'll have to call the police. They will probably be more than a little happy about the information I could give them. The girl is still in the back. I gave her some supplies to last a few days. I figure once you sober up, you could take care of her.
> Don't try anything stupid. I will have the last laugh.
> Your pal, Jennifer
> P.S. Sidney says, "Hello"

Eddie grabbed the closest thing to him, which happened to be a lamp, and smashed it against the wall. Rushing into the bedroom he saw that the money was gone. He got the tape recorder and started to listen. Forty minutes later the tape player recorded the closing of the door as Jennifer and Sidney left the trailer.

Savannah information did not reveal a listing for Mary Lou Pratt. He conducted a search on his computer without any luck. Thirty minutes and three beers later, Eddie went from being in shock to boiling mad. He always had the attitude of a killer. Now he had the motivation. He would rather be dead than let them get away with this. Eddie continued on into the night in his drunken rage. Sometime in the early morning he passed out. By sheer determination Eddie dragged himself out of bed and went to work the next morning. He didn't want to raise suspicion so he had to show up for work.

~

Jennifer and Sidney arrived in Savannah on Monday evening. By 8:30 that evening they knocked on Mary Lou Pratt's door.

A forty-five year old bleached blond wearing a mini-skirt and a tank top came to the door. "Yes," she said.

"Sidney Lawton," he said reaching out his hand, "We did some partying in North Myrtle."

"I did a lot of partying in North Myrtle. You do look vaguely familiar."

"How about a five-day drunken, pot-smoking orgy," Sidney thought. "We spent some time in that big white beach house," he said trying to jog some of the smoke from her brain.

"Oh, yeah. I remember now. You were some kind of an actor right?"

Jennifer managed to choke back a laugh.

"Yeah, right. That was a while ago," Sidney said.

"You told me your next film was with Julia Clarkston. I saw her next film and I didn't see you in it."

Jennifer burst out into a laugh at this point but quickly tried to make it look like she was gagging, which was not much of a stretch.

Waving toward Jennifer, Mary Lou asked, "And this is?"

"Oh, I'm sorry. This is my girl, Jennifer."

"Hello," Mary Lou said as she nodded her way.

Jennifer wondered if she had ever seen a woman more ridiculously dressed. Mary Lou evidently had put on a few pounds over the years and her wardrobe had not quite caught up with that reality.

"Well hey, come on in and have a seat," Mary Lou said. "I got wine, beer or water?"

"Water," they both said.

She brought them some water and herself a beer. She sat down in such a way as to show Sidney all the leg she had.

"So what brings you two dolls to Savannah?"

"We're here on business," Sidney said.

"Oh, and I was hoping this was a social call," Mary Lou said. "Well what can I do for you?"

"We need some new ID's. You still doing any of that?"

"That's all I've ever done. They say I'm the best around."

"I'm sure every man within a hundred miles would have an opinion on that," Jennifer thought.

"Could you fix us up? It has to be solid, husband and wife," Sidney said.

"Movie star on the run. I love it," Mary Lou smiled. "I can fix you up. I don't take credit."

"We got cash, darling. Ain't no problem."

"It will take two days. You're welcome to stay here."

"We have a room, thank you," Jennifer chimed in.

"It will be twenty-two hundred."

"We can handle it," Sidney said as they got up to leave. "We'll be in touch."

"They'll be ready Wednesday."

"Good enough," Sidney said. Mary Lou patted his backside as he stepped out the door.

"She'll be all right for crying out loud. She knows what she's doing," Sidney said as they got in the car.

"I hope so," Jennifer managed. "Julia Clarkston?" she said looking across the car at him. "You're pathetic."

CHAPTER 17

Eddie Britain was not into self-preservation. He was a man driven by whatever demon happened to be on the forefront. At the moment, his reason for living was to find and kill Sidney and Jennifer. He knew that if and when he left Chesterfield, Jennifer would sing. He would go from being an unknown grease monkey to the most wanted man in America. He was willing to take that chance.

His ace in the hole had to be the girl. Killing her would be so easy. As long as she was still alive and in his control he had some leverage. After all, she was his cash cow. He may have to milk her again.

The idea of dragging her around with him was too risky. He had to find a place to keep her for a while. Eddie had just the place in mind. Hopefully he could move her within the week. He would head down to Georgetown this weekend to check things out.

Everyday that week as soon as the sun went down Eddie would go to see Liz. Her temporary hiatus from his terrible attacks came to a sickening end. If it were not for her newfound faith in God she would never have maintained her sanity. She prayed that she could endure and by God's grace, someday forgive.

~

"What do you think, doll?" she said as she gently rubbed her chest against his.

"Ed and June Jones. I like it. You do good work," he said.

"Where you going from here?" she asked as she nibbled on his ear.

"Thinking about going down to the Gulf coast, maybe Pensacola Beach. The beach there is beautiful, whitest sand I've ever seen. We just might head that way."

"If you're ever up this way again you need to come see me. And oh, you can leave her at home."

"I might just do that," he said. He left sometime later.

〜

Jerry sat in his car and read the letter from Liz. He hung his head and cried, "Oh, God, bring her home to me." He tucked the letter into his shirt pocket and drove home. He was thrilled that she was alive but sick over what she might be going through. He prayed that God would protect her.

〜

Jake sat in his easy chair and looked out his back door. He loved to sit and watch the birds. It was Friday night. Tomorrow he planned to pay a visit to Eddie Britain's place. He expected to find Eddie home. His plan was to pose as a local pastor trying to make contacts in the area. He hoped he would get in the door. At this point that possibility seemed remote.

His girlfriend, Sally McSwain, was on the way over. She was picking up a movie and a couple steaks. Jake supplied the beer. He was enjoying her company more and more as the months went by. Up to this point they had not been intimate. Neither one of them felt great about getting physically involved before marriage. Even though that's how they felt, sometimes nature just takes over.

Later that evening, nature took over.

〜

Saturday August eleventh found Eddie heading to Georgetown looking for an old acquaintance, a Mr. Holmes Chamblin. Holmes was a black man who was accused and convicted of raping and killing a white woman outside of Georgetown. While doing time and waiting for his execution, he escaped into the thick swamp area north of Georgetown. Through the years the rumors filled the area that Holmes was alive and lived deep in the uninhabited swamps filled with alligators and snakes of every description.

Eddie, an avid hunter, was deep in that same swamp two years ago. He heard gunshots and the sound of pursuit directly ahead of him.

He witnessed two county sheriff deputies overcome a black man and beat him with their fists and Billie sticks. The man was down and seemed out cold and yet the deputies continued to beat him. Eddie, who had a hatred for the law as long as he could remember, raised his semi-automatic deer rifle and shot them both in the back, ripping huge wounds in their midsections. They died instantly. Killing those officers was more satisfying to Eddie than if he had killed the largest buck in South Carolina.

He checked the pulse of the black man and determined that he was still alive. Eddie wrapped the exposed skin of the black man with strips cut from the deputies clothing. It would be a while before he could get back. To leave the skin exposed to the creatures of the swamp would be suicide. He dragged the dead bodies some one hundred feet from where the black man was lying. In this dense swamp thirty feet was out of sight. He checked the black man again and headed out. It would take him at least five hours to get back. He had to get to the police car and move it. Dogs might be able to track him if they could pick up a scent where the deputies entered the swamp.

The bodies were laid six hundred yards from the gravel logging road where the deputies had parked. The area was one of the most desolate in the state. The roads here might see one vehicle a day. Arriving at the patrol car, Eddie opened the trunk and placed his motor bike inside. He drove the police car six miles along the dirt-logging road not passing another vehicle. Finding a place where he could pull off without leaving any footprints, he got his bike out of the trunk and rode back.

Eddie arrived back to where he had left the black man an hour before dark. He checked him again, built a small fire, and settled in for the night.

The following morning Eddie was up and stirring when he noticed some movement from the man. He was still very weak from the beating he had endured. Weak and terrified he fixed his eyes on Eddie Britain not uttering a word. Eddie's stare bore through him.

"Those pigs did their best to kill you last night. What did you do, steal a watermelon?" Eddie sneered.

The black man didn't bat an eye as he stared at the sinister-looking young white man.

"Those boys were trying to kill you. Ain't no doubt in my mind. I had to teach them a lesson."

Eddie studied him. He still didn't speak. "I saved your ass. You can at least speak to me." He knelt in front of him and tapped him in the chest. "What's your name? If you're running from the law I just killed two of them. The law means nothing to me. What's your name?"

"Holmes," he said. "Holmes Chamblin. Thank you's sir."

"What are you doing in the swamp?"

"I lives here."

"You live in this place? You got to be kidding?"

He shook his head that he wasn't kidding. "Lives here seventeen years. Back in there 'bout seven miles."

Eddie Britain looked at him in astonishment. He knew the swamp got even more unforgiving the farther you went in. He had never ventured more than three miles from the road and he had never known anyone else to go even that far. "He's on the run," he thought.

"I guess you don't have many visitors."

"Never no visitors, Jes me, the swamp, and my ol' woman. Dat's all I needs."

"How often you come to town?"

"Whenever I's gets a mess of gator's hides. I's come in and trades them for stuff I need. Maybe two times a year."

"You're on the run, ain't ya?" Eddie ventured.

Holmes Chamblin commenced to tell the story that led up to his living in the swamp. When he finished Eddie knew that if he ever needed a big favor, or if he ever needed to get away, he need not look any farther than Holmes.

On this basis, Eddie set out to find the whereabouts of Holmes Chamblin.

Jake woke up Saturday morning with Sally curled up on the other side of the bed. They had been seeing each other for eleven months. They had both been very cautious. This new physical development would certainly change the equation.

Jake thought that after the death of his wife he might not ever be with another woman in an intimate way. It was not what either one of them had intended. Most likely there would be no going back.

Jake stepped out of bed, pulled on some clothes and made some coffee. After they shared breakfast Jake put on his well-worn black suit. He looked the part of a dirt poor country preacher.

He gave Sally a kiss and said, "I'll call you tonight." He was more than a little nervous as he stepped out the door.

"Be careful," she said with her eyes full of concern.

Jake got into his old truck and reflected on how long it had been since any woman had really cared about him. He remembered how important it had always been to him. It seemed like it was in another life. Sally brought those memories back.

The directions to Eddie Britain's place were simple enough. Twenty minutes later and he was within a half mile of his destination. His hands were sweaty with perspiration. Passing as a country preacher should not be a problem. What concerned him most was how Eddie would react, especially if he suspected anything.

The area was extremely desolate. Dwellings were miles apart. Before long Eddie's doublewide trailer came into view. There was no activity on the premises. A couple of old vehicles that looked like they had not been running for several years were in the yard. He pulled into the drive, turned off the engine and listened. A pack of large dogs were barking somewhere behind the house. He sat in his car a few moments to be sure the dogs were contained. A minute later he was knocking on the front door with his Bible in hand.

He knocked again, nothing. He looked in the side window and could see that the inside was not well kept. Eddie was supposed to have some kind of girlfriend, a former stripper was what Jake had heard. No one was home. Jake gently checked the front door. It was locked. He walked around the trailer and found the back door locked. The dogs barking some one hundred yards behind him made him a bit nervous.

Jake had walked around the trailer several times and was getting ready to leave when he noticed that a bedroom window was slightly ajar. He scooted a barrel to the window, climbed up on top of it and gave the window a pull. It opened easily. He looked around and carefully stepped inside.

His palms were sweating and his knees were shaking. This was just a little more thrilling than carrying mail. The place wasn't clean but it wasn't filthy either. It looked like it could have had a woman's touch at one time. The dining room table was covered with dirty dishes and beer bottles. There was a garbage can sitting in the living room that was overflowing with beer cans. Jake noticed that all the cans were the same brand. They either drank the same beer, or the girl had split.

To say that he was nervous would be an understatement. He continually looked out the front window for any sign of someone coming. After a few minutes the dogs stopped barking. He walked into the bedroom and looked around. It became apparent that the girl had left when he saw two dressers and one of them was completely empty. Also, only half the closet had clothes in it. Looking through the dirty clothes Jake found some under garments that certainly did not belong to Eddie. She must have left in a hurry.

Being careful not to leave anything different, Jake went through every drawer and every cabinet in the house. He noticed a couch that looked like it had been used a lot. From the way it was sagging, it could have been the sleeping quarters for a large person, probably a male. Of course, that was only speculation. Evidently Eddie did not believe in keeping good records because Jake could not find any important papers. The only thing that he did find was some mail. Most of it addressed to Eddie Britain, but some of it went to a Jennifer Skaggs. He stuck a piece of her junk mail in his pocket.

After forty-five minutes in the trailer, Jake climbed out the back window. When he hit the ground his breathing went back to normal. He could bluff his way out if he was discovered outside of the trailer.

He quietly began to sneak back toward the lot where he had heard the dogs barking. He moved with caution. They were not barking as he edged closer. Sixty feet from the lot, Jake stood behind a large willow tree and looked onto the lot. He could see five large rottweilers in the sixty-by-sixty lot. It seemed odd that anyone would have that many large dogs. The cost of feeding them had to be considerable. It was also odd that the dogs were caged up. There was not another human being within a mile or so from here. What good could they be doing caged up in the lot?

In the center of the lot was a small cement block building. Evidently it was the doghouse. From where Jake was standing he could not see where the dogs could enter. There was a regular door facing the road but it was padlocked. The padlock seemed odd also. It was not like anyone would come into that pen to steal anything. After a few moments Jake slowly backed away from the lot and returned to his car. Ninety minutes after his arrival Jake headed back to Myrtle Beach.

Liz had listened intensely as the dogs barked. Obviously a person that they did not know had been in the area. She knew that if she cried out and Eddie heard her he would certainly kill her.

If she had only known how close her freedom had been.

CHAPTER 18

Eddie arrived in Georgetown around six on Friday night. He headed to a few of the local dives in the city asking about Holmes. Very few people even knew who he was talking about let alone where he might be. He called on a couple of acquaintances but had no luck there either. Around 8:00 p.m. he stopped at a café by the river for a beer and hamburger. Two hours and several beers later he headed out the door. He walked around the downtown area until 11:30. The hot muggy day was getting some relief thanks to a nighttime breeze.

Getting into his car he drove a few miles south to a joint called Abraham's Roadhouse. The Roadhouse had long been the favorite hang out and pick up joint of the black community. Eddie had to be just a little crazy to walk into this place. Fortunately for Eddie he was more than a little crazy. He stepped out of his car and surveyed the scene.

It was Friday night and the place was packed. Outside the front door stood a group of about twenty men and women who were mostly under thirty. The men were athletic looking with bulging muscles. The women were dressed so as to get a response from any male breathing.

Eddie drew a deep breath and scooted through the door like he knew what he was doing. He had only been here once before when a black girl had been paying him some attention and he made the mistake of coming here looking for her. Some of the brothers took offense. Tonight he was definitely in the look but not touch mode.

Inside the joint was packed. Except for two or three women, he was the only other Caucasian in the place. He made his way to the bar and ordered a large draft. The place was designed to hold 200 people but there were at least 350 inside. A hot blues band was playing and the dance floor was crowded beyond capacity. Eddie sipped his beer and scanned the crowd for a familiar face. Several women were giving him the eye. "Not tonight," he thought.

When a barstool opened he took a seat and downed another beer. He was finished with his second beer when a hand poked him on the shoulder. Next to him was a large black man about thirty years old. Eddie was sure he had met him somewhere before.

"Hey man, what you doin' in here? You must want to get killed or somethin," the man laughed.

"Where do I know you from?" Eddie asked.

"I work over at the mill on the docks. You remember me. Come on now. You remember Jamaul now, don't you?"

"Yeah, I remember. You worked afternoons. You worked with that huge dude."

Jamaul laughed, "Oh yeah, Chester Brown. Now there's a big man." He reared back studying Eddie and said, "I bet you're lookin for a little African American action? Am I right?"

"Well there's plenty to be had. No, actually I'm looking for an old friend. I thought maybe he might be here. I'm sorry, the name is Eddie. Eddie Britain," he said as he held out his hand.

"Eddie, I thought your name was something like that. Why don't you come on over to our table. You might live through the night over there," he howled as the two men grabbed their beer and moved on over.

They settled at a corner rectangular table where they joined three men and three women. Sobriety was a long gone concept at this table. Jamaul introduced everyone. They all acknowledged Eddie's presence and continued getting drunker and louder.

"Where you working now?" Jamaul asked.

"I'm up at Myrtle Beach. I work in maintenance at this ritzy gated community called Chesterfield. You talk about a bunch of uppity white folks."

"Chesterfield? That's where Liz Alton was living. It's been in the papers almost every day. She used to live around here."

"I didn't know her," was all Eddie said.

After a few more beers even Eddie was getting drunk. Sometime around two in the morning, Eddie managed to ask Jamaul if he had ever heard of Holmes Chamblin.

Jamaul put down his beer and gazed at Eddie. "Yeah, I know Holmes. What you want with Holmes?"

"We're indebted to each other. Let's put it that way. I saved his life a few years ago. He was very appreciative. I need a favor from him now."

"How's he gonna help you? He lives in the swamp. He ain't got a pot to pee in."

"Do you know where he's at?"

"Nobody knows where Holmes is at. His mamma don't even know."

"I gotta find him."

"You gonna be here tomorrow?" Jamaul asked.

"Yeah, I'll be in town."

"Meet me at the River Bridge at noon."

"I'll be there."

"Come on, white boy," Jamaul said. "Let me get you to your car while you can still walk."

Jamaul guided Eddie through the thinned out crowd and walked him to his car. "Go," was all he said.

Meanwhile at the table, Skoo Stackpole drank his last beer, grabbed his favorite lady, and headed for the door.

Eddie's head was splitting as he sat in his car at the pull off at the south end of the River Bridge. The August sun was relentless as the noon hour approached. Occasionally a slight breeze would bring some relief to the low country terrain. Eddie's rough living was beginning to take its toll. His diet, normally poor, had become terrible since Jennifer had left. It consisted mostly of beer and bologna. A few slow-moving barefooted locals meandered across the bridge. Nobody was in a hurry on this hot day.

Out of the blue Jamaul opened the passenger side and sat down. After a quick glance at Eddie he lit an unfiltered cigarette. Jamaul's life consisted of hard work, simple pleasures and a few beers at the Roadhouse.

"Pretty darn odd you coming all the way down here to find Holmes. Ain't many people in this town that would even believe he was alive, let alone come down to find him." He drew a long hot drag on his cigarette and stared at the lazy river. He looked at Eddie with hard eyes, "I guess you think you're a tough guy? You mess with Holmes, and you'll end up floating in that river."

"I ain't gonna mess with him. I told you. We have a mutual understanding."

"You need to hide something. Is that it?"

"Could be," Eddie said.

"I know where he is. I'm gonna take you to him. If you stiff him, it will be your last day on earth. Understand?"

Eddie never took well to being spoken down to. He bit his tongue and managed to quell his inner rage. "I understand," was all he said.

"Get out of the car," Jamaul said. He motioned Eddie to walk directly away from the river. They walked past three or four mill houses and went to the back door of a small white house on the adjoining street. "You wait here. I'll be right back," he told Eddie.

Several minutes later, Jamaul came to the back door, opened the screen and told Eddie to come in. He was taken through the kitchen and into the living room. In the living room he found Holmes sitting on the sofa. Three large black men and two women were also there. Jamaul motioned for Eddie to take a seat.

Eddie felt like he could handle himself in most situations, but any man in this room, including Holmes, could kill him with his bare hands.

Holmes was not happy to see Eddie Britain. Holmes was appreciative that Eddie had saved his life, but he also knew Eddie to be a cold-blooded killer. He was not the kind of person to whom one needed to owe a favor.

"Holmes, I guess you remember me?" Eddie ventured.

Holmes nodded.

"I really appreciate you seeing me. I got a favor to ask. It's kind of personal though. Could we talk in private?"

Holmes looked at him with the eyes of a man who trusted very few people. "These peoples are my friends. I's trust 'em with my life."

"I can appreciate that. I really can. Tell you what, let me talk to you in private. You just give me a yes or no. That'll be the end of it. We can talk in the bedroom. I can't try anything. There's no way out. I gotta come through here. This white boy might be stupid but he ain't crazy."

A large black man got down in Eddie's face. "Dumb, man you're dumb. You know that? He said we're family here. His business is our business."

Holmes grabbed him on the shoulder, "Back off. . . . In here," he said to Eddie motioning to an adjoining room.

They entered a small bedroom that was occupied by a sleeping young woman. "She's alright," Holmes said motioning toward the girl. "She's out fo the evening."

Holmes sat on the bed and motioned for Eddie to take a seat in a small chair by the dresser. Holmes then gave him a look that said, 'What's this about?'

"I need a big favor. I need you to keep a girl for me for a while. She needs to disappear. She shouldn't be any trouble. A white gal, good looking. You might even enjoy having her around," he said with his sinister smile.

"Always been jest me and my ol' woman. Never no one else."

"I know, I know, man. I wouldn't ask, but I really need the favor."

"How long do I's needs to keeps her?"

"Shouldn't be long, a few months tops."

"What's da' woman think of this?"

"She's not happy about it but she ain't got no gripe. She knows damn well things could be worse, a whole lot worse."

"What's in it fo' me?"

"Hey man, you owe me. I saved your ass. You'd be dead now or worse. I got a little money, not a lot. I should be able to get you a few hundred. Come on man, you owe me this one. Guys like us, we gotta stick together. You know I'm telling you straight."

Holmes was a hunted man yet he lived his life with a high code of honor. He did not like Eddie Britain, but the man did save his life. He did owe him. No doubt there was some sinister reason for Eddie to want him to keep the girl. To tell Eddie no would be more of a risk than he cared to take. His woman would not be pleased but she would have to live with it.

"I's leavin fo' the swamp tomorrow evening. Can you's have her here?"

"No problem," Eddie smiled. "I can't bring her to this house though. No one else can know. Its gotta be that way."

"Dees are my brothers, my family," Holmes said.

"I can't take that chance. You got to understand, man. I know you don't take unnecessary chances."

If there was one thing that Holmes could understand it was the importance of being careful. This was the town that he grew up in, the town where he had at least sixty relatives, and yet only this small handful of people knew for sure that he was alive. And even at that, no one knew where he lived. He sensed the same kind of urgency and caution in Eddie.

"Brings her to where you saved me. Da place where you killed the police. Have her there an hour befo' dark."

"I'll be there with the girl. Thanks," he said as he got up and left.

Holmes showed him to the door and he was gone.

CHAPTER 19

Eddie got back to the trailer Saturday evening. He downed several beers and made his pilgrimage to the dog lot to see Liz. Like so many nights before, she cried herself to sleep. Little did she know but her life was about to take a dramatic turn.

The next day at 4:30 p.m. Eddie dropped in unexpectedly on Liz. She had been reading her Bible.

"You don't really believe that stuff do you?" he snarled.

"Of course I do," she said in a near whisper.

"Well now, sweet thing, your prayers are about to be answered. You're going on a trip today. Get your things together. I'll be back in two hours."

Eddie left as abruptly as he came in. Liz's heart was beating like a drum. The prospect of leaving this hellhole was almost beyond belief. Even to go to her death would be better than staying in this place she tried to tell herself. Getting her things together would take every bit of five minutes. She sat in the dark the next two hours alternating between crying and praying. Whatever God had in store for her, she was ready to take the next step.

Two hours later, the door flew open. "You ready to travel, darling?"

She stood up holding a small box containing all her worldly belongings. Eddie took her by her belt loop and led her through the dog lot. The dogs were all around her. They were the most ferocious animals she had ever seen. It was the first time she had been out of the building. She thanked God that she had made it this far.

He led her to the back of the trailer and had her sit in a swing that was cemented in place. He secured her leg to one of the legs of the swing with a heavy nylon cord.

"I'll be back in a few minutes, darling. I gotta check on a few things."

Knowing that escape was futile, she tried to relax and enjoy the beauty of the world around her. The swampland of South Carolina had never looked so good. To Liz it was one of the most beautiful sights she had ever seen. Though impossible to figure how at this point, Liz was positive that God was answering her prayers. Her strong faith would see her through whatever lay ahead.

Eddie went to his secret stash and pulled out 2,900 dollars from inside an old shoe. He was going to have to make it last. He was not planning on coming back. After dropping Liz off, he would head for Savannah to find Mary Lou Pratt. He was quite sure that Sidney and Jennifer were long gone from Savannah and he was equally sure they would leave a trail. Intelligence was not one of their strong suits. He smiled at the prospect of killing them both.

He walked out the front door and opened the trunk of his car. It was going to be one hot ride for Liz.

"Sorry, darling," he said as he wrapped duct tape around her hands, feet and mouth. "We're looking at about a forty-minute drive. I don't think it will kill you. You try anything cute on the trip down and you're dead. Do you understand? I knew you would," he said as he manhandled her into the trunk.

The trip down was rough and hot. A person prone to panic could have easily suffocated in the hot trunk. Liz hung on knowing that it was only temporary. Whatever was ahead could not be any worse than what she had already been through, or would it? She would soon find out.

Eddie took his time getting there. The last thing he needed was trouble with the law. Traffic was light on this Sunday afternoon. He arrived at his destination forty-five minutes before he was supposed to meet Holmes. The walk back to meet Holmes would take thirty minutes. He opened the trunk and saw Liz drenched with perspiration.

Liz looked around in amazement. "This guy's got a thing for the remote," she thought.

Eddie led her into the woods. Thirty minutes later they were at their destination. Eddie knew exactly where he had left the officers' bodies.

"We're going to be parting ways for a while. I really have enjoyed your company. I know Holmes will take good care of you till I get back," he grinned. "You're going to like Holmes."

"Who is Holmes?" she thought.

From twenty feet behind them, a strong African voice said, "I sees you made it."

Startled, Liz turned quickly. Standing before her was a large black man, probably in his early forties. He was six feet tall and weighed at least two hundred pounds. He looked completely at home in the deep swamp.

"Hey dude, you liked to scared me. How long you been back there?"

"Few minutes."

"This is Liz. She ain't gonna give you any trouble. If she does, kill her. Here's your money," he said as he handed Holmes three hundred dollars. Holmes slowly counted it.

"When will you be coming out again? I mean, I don't expect you to keep the girl forever."

"I usually comes up afa Christmas. Stay a few days, leaves befo' New Years."

Eddie figured that gave him four and a half months. Should be long enough.

"Can I meet you here on New Years Eve, same time?"

"You's have to meet me the day afa Christmas. I's can't take the girl into town."

"Of course, about this time of day?"

"Noon better," Holmes said.

"I'll see you then, and thanks Holmes. I know you'll take real good care of her. I bet you like a little white action every now and then."

Eddie looked at Liz and said, "You be nice to my friend now. I will be seeing you again. I know you'll count the hours," he sneered as he headed back toward the road. He turned and added, "Oh, it wouldn't be a good idea for her to just walk out of here. That might bring in a few cops. You do understand don't you, Holmes?" Eddie turned and left.

Liz stood petrified. What would happen now? There was absolutely no way of escape. She could never outrun this man and she would be hard pressed to hurt him. She stood still, barely breathing.

"Dees woods very dangerous. You stay rights behind me. You understands me?" Holmes said with the authority of a man who knew what he was talking about.

"Yes sir," Liz managed as she picked up her box of belongings and followed.

After about thirty minutes and a half mile, they stopped on a dry knoll to make camp. Holmes busied himself making a small fire. Liz sat and watched as he prepared their camp for the evening.

He pulled a Mason jar of stew from his pack, warmed it over the fire and drew some water for them from a near by spring.

He handed her some stew and water then bowed his head and gave thanks.

"A very good sign," Liz thought. They ate in silence.

The night was pitch black except for the glowing embers of the disappearing fire. Holmes reached into his sack and pulled out a worn thin blanket and handed it to Liz.

"You sleep. Holmes not gonna hurt you. You sleep now," he said.

There was a kindness in his voice that removed any fear. Despite being in the middle of a snake-infested swamp with a man she barely knew, she managed to fall off to sleep, but not before thanking God and praying for Jerry and for her safe return to him.

CHAPTER 20

After giving Sally a call, Jake dialed Rudy's home phone.

"Hello," Rudy barked.

"Just reporting in," Jake said.

"Darn, you made it back. I was just getting ready to call Sally to see if there was anything I could do."

"I can always count on you. I got back a couple hours ago. There wasn't anyone there. I looked the place over. Looks a lot like a bachelor pad, at least right now it does. I think his gal has split. Her name is Jennifer Skaggs. Her name was on several pieces of mail. There might have been someone else there. It looked like the sofa could have been home to a large male. That's just a hunch."

"Nothing really out of the ordinary?" Rudy asked.

"Not really, just low life living. He has a dog lot back behind the house. It had five or six rottweilers in there. They looked vicious. I would hate to have to feed that pack of blood-thirsty animals. That seemed a little odd. I guess I could see it if they were running free to guard the place, you know. But locked in a pen like that? It seems to me like that's throwing good money away."

"Why don't you stop by the station tomorrow. We'll run some info on this Jennifer Skaggs and see what comes up. Maybe we can stop by and see Jill for lunch."

"Now that sounds like a plan. Is ten okay? . . . Good, see ya then," Jake said as he hung up the phone and turned on the TV. Ten minutes later he was heading for Sally's house. He had it bad.

~

Liz awoke shortly after dawn to find Holmes cooking some kind of small animal he had captured during the night. It looked like there were three of them in the pan.

"Dey will be ready in a few minutes. Ders a small spring right o'r der if you wants to clean up."

"Thank you," Liz said. She wandered over to the cool flowing water. Looking behind her, she noticed to Holmes's credit that he was not trying to sneak a peek. She removed her shoes and splashed water on her arms and face as her feet dangled in the spring. Fifteen minutes later, she was back at the camp and enjoying breakfast, complete with some instant coffee.

"Holmes, I do appreciate your kindness, I really do. But I don't have any idea what is happening to me or where I'm going. What is going to happen to me?"

Holmes wiped his mouth with a cloth and said, "You's gonna live with me and my woman fo a while. Dat's all. We's not gonna hurt you. We be home des afternoon. We will talk mo den. No mo talk now. Eat please."

"But . . ." Liz started to say as Holmes cut her off. There would be no more talking now. After breakfast they broke camp and headed out through the harshest terrain that Liz had ever seen or imagined.

Only Holmes's keen knowledge of the area kept them alive. Liz counted fifteen alligators and that was before noon. She lost track of the number of snakes she saw. Even with Holmes's expert lead there were several places where they both had to swim. Liz considered herself to be in pretty good shape, but if it were not for the trees to cling to, she probably couldn't have made it without help. Sometime around noon they reached a high place and rested for about an hour. According to Holmes they had two more hours to go.

~

Jake dragged himself out of Sally's bed about 9. After a cup of coffee he was off to the Myrtle Beach Police Department to see Rudy. He felt compelled to call Jerry Swanson whenever he had a chance. The guy had to feel like his world was falling apart. With every day that passed his chances of seeing his wife alive again diminished. Thankfully Jake did not have to drive all the way to King's Highway to get to the police station. He turned into the business district and on to Oak Street. The locals usually stayed clear of the tourist section during the summer unless they had no choice. Even on Monday morning the traffic was heavy this time of year.

"Me no speaky English," Jake smiled as he stuck his head into Rudy's small office.

"Hey, Jake," Rudy said without looking up.

"What we got?"

Rudy picked up a report and looked at Jake, "Being the socialite you are, you probably know this girl. She's a stripper here at the beach. Or at least she used to be. I guess she's been playing house with our boy for a while." He tossed Jake the report complete with a promotional photo of her working days.

"Nice looking chick," Jake observed. "Sweet Buns, now that's an original name."

"Isn't it though," Rudy said. "Her last job was at the Stallion Club out on 501. Left there about eighteen months ago."

"How do you figure? Dynamite looking chick like this gets tied up with a loser like Eddie Britain. Especially when there are nice guys like you and me under every bush," Jake added. "Have you called the club?"

"Yeah, talked to the manager. Said he barely remembered her. I guess with all those naked young women coming through it's hard to keep up."

"Believe me, I know where he's coming from," Jake said.

"You been drinking this morning?" Rudy asked Jake. "Let's go, I wanna check with Josh. He's been developing the pictures we got from the surveillance cameras at the mall. Let's see if today is our lucky day."

Josh Clark's office was two doors down. He had been with the department eleven years, the last seven as the photography expert.

"Josh, old boy. How's the garden doing?" Rudy said as he and Jake barged in.

"Don't start with me, Rudy."

"Oh, please, don't tell me your tomatoes rotted again this year?" Rudy could be a real wise guy.

"What do you want, Rogers. Some of us have to work for a living."

"For starters, this is Jake Brown, my friend and part-time sleuth."

Josh gave Jake a quick handshake. "If you're his friend you are a rare bird indeed."

"Speaking of work, let's see if this local beauty matches up with any of our mall pictures," Rudy said as he slid Josh the picture of Jennifer.

Josh expertly positioned the picture into his scanner and captured a digital copy. He then downloaded it to his photo file and began to pull the mall images up on his twenty-inch computer screen.

There were four women that were remote possibilities. Three of them after a little deliberation were eliminated. The last one got their attention.

"I tell you what, it is a possibility," Josh said.

Rudy added, "The hair has a different look, and of course the wardrobe."

"Being the cultured guy that I am, I would say that 'Sweet Buns' dresses up real nice," Jake chirped in.

"Sweet Buns?" Josh asked.

"Most strippers don't use their real name, Einstein," Rudy said. "Could you get us a zoom on that profile, especially the nose and eyes?"

Josh fidgeted with the controls and brought the two profiles together. He sat in his chair and stared at the screen. "Gentlemen, I think we have a winner." He leaned back in his chair and looked at Rudy, "Where's she at?"

"That's just it, we don't know. Jake just did some sneaking around her supposed dwelling. She doesn't seem to be living there anymore."

"Where was she living?"

"She lived with a local punk named Eddie Britain. Total lack of class kind of guy. And guess what? The jerk works out at Chesterfield. He's part of the maintenance crew," Rudy said.

Josh pulled a slide up that showed Jennifer and Sidney together at the table and said, "I take it this dude is not Britain?"

Rudy shook his head in agreement. "No, it's not. It could be our pick-up guy. There are some similarities. Blow his face up and see if we have a match."

"It makes sense. The pick-up guy would have to be an unknown. Otherwise, the game is over," Josh stated as he brought the images together. All eyes were glued to the screen as the picture showed a startling resemblance.

"I believe this party needs to move to Chesterfield," Rudy said as they headed for the door. "Bertha," he said to the receptionist, "I need a search warrant for Eddie Britain's place on Skinner Road, pronto."

"Yes sir," she said. "Give me an hour."

They hurried out the door.

When the trio arrived at Chesterfield they rushed into maintenance supervisor Lenny Ragozzi's office and found him sipping coffee with the gatehouse floozy, Shirley.

"What's the problem, boys?" Lenny asked as they walked in.

"We need to speak to Eddie Britain."

"Eddie's not here. First day that boy's missed in I don't know when."

The men looked around at each other. "Did he call in?" Josh asked.

"I haven't heard from him. I called his house but didn't get an answer."

"Doesn't that seem kind of odd?" Rudy asked.

"Under normal circumstances, yes. But you got to understand that in this business reliable help is hard to come by. The kid hasn't missed many days. I'm not gonna fire him over missing one day."

"What you pretty boys want with Eddie?" Shirley chimed in with her usual sultry voice.

"We need to talk to him," Rudy said.

"What you boys doing now, arresting people for hustling the women around here?" Shirley asked as she exposed most of her legs to the attentive men.

"Just need to ask him some questions, that's all," Josh said.

Lenny Ragozzi scratched his considerable girth, "You don't think he's tied up with this Liz Swanson deal, do you? He's a strange bird, I'll grant you that. But the boy couldn't be involved with something like that. No way."

"If he shows up give us a call," Rudy said on the way out the door.

They swung by the station and picked up the search warrant. With five more men and three additional cruisers they headed to Eddie's place. Not getting an answer at the door, they picked the lock and went in.

Thirty minutes of going over the place with a fine tooth comb came up with nothing. Officers were also scanning the exterior looking for anything that could prove helpful. Twenty minutes into the search, FBI agent Homer

Southard arrived acting like his usual belligerent self.

"Sergeant," Deputy Larry Carpenter addressed Rudy. "We need to check the dog lot out back. Those dogs are vicious. Lance is here and he's ready to drug them. Just waiting for the word."

"Do it," Rudy said.

"What is this bull about, Rogers?" Homer Southard grunted. "You don't spit without me knowing about it. You got that?"

"Happened kind of quick, Homer. You know how it can be sometimes," Rudy said. He was thinking, "I'd love to see my foot planted in his rear."

Larry Carpenter was at the door. "Rudy, you need to see this," he said as he hurriedly led them to the dog lot.

"My God," was all Rudy could manage as he stared into what had been Liz Swanson's home for months.

"My boys are going over this place. I want nothing touched," FBI agent Southard said. "Maybe we can get lucky."

Jake and Rudy turned to walk away. Rudy went to the car phone and called headquarters for more help. He ordered an "All Points Bulletin" for Eddie Britain and Jennifer Skaggs.

His fingers nervously dialed Jerry Swanson's number. Twenty-five minutes later Jerry was at the scene.

CHAPTER 21

Five and a half hours through terrible snake-infested terrain brought Liz and Holmes to their destination. In the middle of a thicket of moss-covered willows, surrounded on all sides by water, stood a small, crude dwelling made entirely of natural materials. The building itself was off the ground about five feet even though the spot did seem to be dry. One hundred feet from the building Holmes turned to Liz and said, "You wait."

Several minutes passed after Holmes went into the crude dwelling. Holmes came out on to the porch followed by a slim black woman with pretty features, probably in her late thirties.

They stood on the porch and Holmes motioned Liz to come forward. She waded through the swamp and got to the dry ground where the shanty stood. Holmes remained on the porch as the woman came to meet Liz.

"My name is Osa," the woman said as she extended her hand.

"Liz," she said. "Liz Swanson."

The woman obviously had no idea who Liz was. News in this place was non-existent. Osa had plenty of intelligence and conducted herself in a refined manner. How this woman could end up in a place like this was a mystery to Liz. "It must be love," she thought.

"My man tells me that you'll be with us for a while. First company we've ever had here." Osa looked over her shoulder toward Holmes and looked back toward Liz. "He's a good man. The best man I've ever known. He treats me real good. Even a good man can fall. Don't tempt him. He's a good man, but he's a man. He could be weak. If you mess with my man, you're going to be out there in that swamp alone. You get the picture?"

"Yes I do," Liz said. "I understand completely. I would say the same thing if I were in your place."

Osa looked at Liz and gave her a genuine smile. "It really is nice to have some company. Come on, I'll show you your space."

Holmes smiled broadly as the two women climbed up on the deck.

Inside the small dwelling were several makeshift chairs, a table, and a sink cut out of a log. The house had one large room and one adjacent bedroom. Open windows surrounded them in every direction. Liz couldn't help but think how homey this primitive structure was. It reminded her of something from the old jungle movies. God was certainly smiling Liz's way.

"You can sleep here for now," Osa said pointing toward a homemade couch in the big room. "I think you will be able to sleep on it. We will fix up some makeshift walls for you before long so you can have some privacy."

Tears welled up in Liz's eyes as Osa took a vase of wild flowers from the window over the sink and put them in the window over the couch that Liz would be sleeping on.

Liz hugged Osa and whispered a sincere "Thank you," in her ear.

Sensing the terror that Liz had endured, Osa said, "Everything's gonna be fine here, honey. I promise. God has given us this heaven on earth and He has brought you to us. His ways are always perfect."

Liz could barely stand as the tears of thanksgiving flowed down her cheeks.

～

"Look at that white sand and aqua water. That's the prettiest beach I've ever seen," Jennifer said to Sidney as they were driving down the beach road twenty miles from Pensacola Beach.

"What did I tell ya, baby? Old Sid's a straight shooter. You're gonna love being a jet setter around here. Let the good times roll!"

Sidney Lawton remembered this area from his days in the Navy when he was stationed at the Pensacola Air Station ten years before.

They arrived at the beach just before dark and checked in at the Gulf Hilton as Ed and June Jones. Tomorrow was a big day. They would be looking for an ocean front condo to buy. Crime was paying real well.

They spent the next week looking at various properties in the area. They finally settled on a spacious three-bedroom condo located on the seventh floor of a new luxury development. The unit came complete with a Jacuzzi and a spacious deck. The purchase was made from a Montgomery couple that was parting company. They had very expensive tastes in furnishings and amenities. They got it all, completely furnished, for just less than four hundred thousand, cash of course.

~

Eddie arrived in Savannah and immediately started hitting all the low life dives and sleazy looking places he could find. Mary Lou Pratt had to be the kind of person who either frequented these places or was known in them. After all, she was a friend of Sidney's. Needless to say, Eddie didn't bother to check with the Chamber of Commerce. After eight hours of looking he got lucky. A drunk not only told him where she lived but he even drove with Eddie to her residence. After giving the drunk a few bucks and dropping him off at the nearest pub, Eddie went a calling.

Not one to shun mixing business with pleasure, Eddie was pleasantly surprised when Mary Lou came to the door wearing spandex pants two sizes too small and a short tank top. She was a bleached blond and was drunk to boot.

"Somebody told me there was a party here tonight," Eddie said as she opened the door.

"Well now, who would have said that?" she said obviously not offended.

"Some guy down on River Road. I'm sorry if I'm wrong, ma'am. I'm new in town and was looking for a little entertainment. Don't mean nothing by it."

"Come on in, darling. I could use some company myself," she said pulling him in the door.

Ten o'clock the next morning Eddie stumbled out of bed. Mary Lou was still dead to the world. The place stunk so bad it even nauseated Eddie. Week old dishes were in the sink. The place had three cats, and who knows how many empty liquor containers were littering the place. Eddie got a cold beer from the refrigerator, picked up the morning paper from the stoop, went out to the back deck and propped his feet up. The bold type article on the front page made him spray his beer all over himself.

"Suspects Identified in Liz Swanson Case" the headline exploded complete with a recent picture of Eddie, Jennifer and the disguised Sidney. The article went on to describe how Eddie worked at the Chesterfield development. His girlfriend Jennifer was seen at the mall on the day of the ransom payoff talking with an alleged accomplice. Britain and Skaggs have since vacated their residence and are on the run. They might not be traveling together and are considered armed and very dangerous. The article gave a brief description of the case and noted that state and federal officials were involved in the case.

There was little doubt that Mary Lou, even with numerous brain cells gone, would easily recognize Eddie and Jennifer from these pictures.

He stuck the paper in his back pocket and went out to the street and pulled his car behind Mary Lou's house.

"Making yourself at home aren't you, doll?" she said standing at the back door screen.

"Yeah, I just thought I'd pull it back here and maybe wash it after bit," he said.

"Don't get too cozy. I don't take in boarders," she said as she headed for the bathroom.

She started the shower and stepped in.

Twenty minutes later she emerged from the shower and saw Eddie sitting with his back to her at the dining room table.

"I mean it, Eddie. You're going to have to split. I don't take in boarders. That's always been my policy," she said drying her hair. Eddie turned to face her and pointed a nine-millimeter straight at her stomach.

"What the. . . . What are you doing?" was all she could manage.

"I need time to think and maybe a favor or two. You don't mind if I take a few minutes, do you? I hate being rushed."

"Sure man. Ain't no problem. Anything, anything. Just name it."

"I need an ID. And I need it now. I hope you can help me. I hate being disappointed."

"Sure. Sure thing," she said pulling out a shoebox from the back of her pantry. "I'm sure we can find something in here. These are all good. Never been used," she said fumbling through the box.

"I need one with blond hair. You got one like that?"

"I'm sure I do. Let me see. . . . Here's one. What do you think?" she said handing a packet of matched ID's to Eddie.

"That will do just fine. Now I need some information. Two friends of mine came through here a couple of weeks ago. Young fellow with a good-looking girlfriend, Sidney and Jennifer, I'm sure you remember them?"

"Sure. They needed some IDs too. They were on their way in a couple days. Didn't stay long."

"What IDs did you give them?"

"I can't tell you that, Eddie. They paid good money for it. I have a reputation to keep up."

Eddie had no doubt that her reputation was well known, especially with every hood in Savannah.

Eddie looked at the barrel of the gun, "I think I told you I hated to be disappointed? Let me ask you again. What name did you give them?"

"It's in my bedroom."

"Well, let's get it. This suspense is more than I can stand," Eddie said as he followed her into the bedroom.

She pulled a small green writing pad from under her mattress and turned to one of the last entries. "Ed and June Jones," she said.

"Very sweet, a married couple. How nice," Eddie mocked. "Where did they go?"

Mary Lou thought a moment, "Pensacola. Pensacola Beach I think he said. You can't tell him where you got this information. He would kill me."

"You can trust me, darling," he said as he started to take off his trousers.

"I'm just not in the mood right now. Come on, Eddie."

"Don't disappoint me now. You know I don't like that."

Realizing that she did not have a choice, she disrobed and lay on the bed. Eddie crawled on top of her. His hands formed around her neck and he began to tighten.

As Mary Lou Pratt gasped her last breath, Eddie looked into her terrified eyes and said, "I've always wanted to do this." She was dead in three minutes.

He got up from the bed and headed into the bathroom. Looking through the cabinet, he found what he was looking for, a blond hair dyeing kit. After shaving off his mustache, he read the directions on the bottle and dyed his hair blond.

Standing in front of the mirror, he had to admit it was a pretty good disguise. Eddie picked up the notebook that contained the entry identifying Ed and June Jones and stuck it in his pocket. He tacked a note on the door that read, "Out of town until Saturday." He figured it would buy him a few days.

"So long Eddie Britain and hello Mike Helms," he said as he headed out the door and started walking. Two miles down the road Eddie called a cab to take him to the bus station. There he purchased a one-way ticket to Atlanta. He would hang around there for a day or two and then get a ticket to Pensacola. He had to always be covering his tracks. By early afternoon Tuesday he was on the road heading for Atlanta.

Chapter 22

"Hello, Linda. Is Mr. Swanson in?" Jake asked at the Swanson estate.

"Yes, he is. It's good to see you again. Please come in. I'll tell him you're here," Linda said as she left the room.

Sitting in this room reminded Jake of the first time he came here. Who would have ever dreamed of the nightmare that was to come? Just a few months ago Jerry Swanson was the most powerful Republican in the state of South Carolina. Now all he could do was try to make it through another day.

"Jake, good to see you," Jerry said as he extended his hand and then sat down in an adjacent chair. "Coffee or tea?" he asked.

"No thanks."

"What brings you out this way?" Jerry asked hoping for some good news but not sensing any.

"I don't really know except to tell you how sorry we all are. I just don't know what we could have done differently. This whole deal with Eddie Britain just did not add up. At least not in time to do any good."

"I appreciate your coming by," Jerry said. "Officer Rogers told me that nothing came up at Britain's place. I guess he took Liz with him."

Jerry continued. "Everyday seems like the worst day of my life. I just don't know how much longer I can stand this. I really don't. I wish I could kill that bastard myself. If only I had insisted that Liz move to Spartanburg with me. I wish I had been home more. I wish I had done a thousand things differently. I just want her home."

"Maybe you could get away for a few days. It might do you some good," Jake offered. "I'm sure Linda can handle this place. You can wait by the phone there as well as you can here."

"I don't know what I'd do without Linda," Jerry said. "She keeps it together while the rest of us are falling apart. She is probably the best paid domestic help in South Carolina and she deserves every penny of it."

"No doubt," Jake agreed.

"I might just head down to the beach house. A few days there might do me some good. I can always think straight down there."

"Edisto?"

"Yeah, Edisto. I guess you guys have those numbers?"

"We've got them. Like I said, you're just a phone call away."

Jerry Swanson shook his head in agreement. He had to get away and he knew it. Maybe the ocean air would help bring back his sanity.

Liz spent her first night on the couch and had a surprisingly good night's sleep. She awoke before Holmes or Osa and went out on the deck to see the dawn arrive. The swamp was alive with activity. The birds and creatures of the swamp were performing a morning serenade. The early morning summer fog was slow to lift from the damp surroundings.

Gazing at the magnificent natural world before her eyes, she could not help but wonder what would be in store for the rest of her life. Only time would tell.

It was a truly amazing place to be. Not a trace of civilization except the occasional sound of an aircraft high overhead. There was something soothing about not having a clock and living completely by nature's timetable. On this beautiful crisp morning Liz's heart was full of thanksgiving. Just two days removed from the dog lot, she had much to be grateful for.

An hour or so later Osa was in the kitchen making coffee that smelled heavenly. She began to fry some kind of fish and wild rice concoction that was as tasty as anything found in a restaurant.

"It smells so good in here," Liz said.

"Thank you," Osa returned. "Coffee is the one thing Holmes has got to bring back whenever he goes to town. Help yourself. Whatever you need is right above the sink. I'll have breakfast ready in a few minutes."

"How often does Holmes go to town?"

"It just depends. Most of the time he goes a couple times a year. Christmas time and mid-summer."

"Good mornin', ladies," Holmes said as he walked into the room and went for the coffeepot.

The three of them enjoyed their breakfast and sat around the deck chatting and watching the wild kingdom unfold before their eyes.

Osa spent an hour reading the Bible to Holmes and Liz. Holmes hung on every word. This woman and man were more in touch with each other and their place in eternity than many of the most learned people in the world. It made Liz reflect on how she had lived the majority of her life. A good life by most people's standards, but in many ways it was a life built on a superficial level. Holmes and Osa could teach most of the people that she knew many of life's most important lessons.

Why would they choose to live in a place like this? Beautiful, yes, but so remote. It was like they were hiding from something. She would find out in her own time. In the meantime she would enjoy every moment away from the hell of the dog lot.

Eddie Britain, alias Mike Helms, arrived in Pensacola on a warm summer afternoon. Arriving by bus, he took a cab to the pier at Pensacola Beach where he enjoyed a beer and looked out over the clear blue water of the Gulf of Mexico. The area was filled with tourists. Most of them were young bikini-clad women. "It's a shame I'm here on business," Eddie thought. "I could learn to enjoy this place."

He saw a small article in the B section of the local paper concerning the Liz Swanson ordeal. He was mentioned briefly as a prime suspect. At this point there was still no link with Mary Lou Pratt in Savannah. He figured that by now the body would be starting to stink and that would draw attention to the house. The police would find his car but would not have a clue as to his whereabouts. Eddie could live with that.

He figured he would look for a job tomorrow. Painters and roofers were always in demand. He'd make some money, hit the bar scene and keep his eyes and ears open. Those two bimbos were bound to show up. They were much too stupid to keep a good cover. Jennifer by now, he was sure, had already secured her place as a first class slut on the beach. She should be showing up before long.

It was doubtful that either would be working. Why should they? They had enough money to live the way they wanted. He was determined to find them before they blew all the money. The thought of killing them was always on his mind. He figured they were carrying the cash with them. He was figuring right.

Ed and June were certainly the toast of the beach. They loved the party. They would frequent their favorite pub and invite a promising table to come to their place for a party that usually lasted all night.

In their sober moments they couldn't help but be concerned about Eddie. Occasionally there would be a story in the local paper about the Swanson affair. Their names were always mentioned and sometimes the article would have a photograph. Luckily, Jennifer, or June as she went by now, had changed her appearance considerably. She was now a blond who loved leather. Sidney's real identity was still unknown.

The thought of Eddie on the loose kept them a little apprehensive even though they figured they were safe. Eddie, after all, had no idea where to look or who to look for.

~

Mike Schaefer had been a letter carrier at the Savannah Post Office for just over nine years. He was in his early thirties and enjoyed his work. Mike had a regular route in a poor part of town, and was known and appreciated in the area. He took pride in doing his job right and he was quick to notice anything amiss in the neighborhood.

At first the foul odor just seemed to blend in with a lot of other foul odors around. And then it started to take on the unmistakable smell of death. He called the police to 103 Carter Lane, the home of a Ms. Mary Lou Pratt.

Officer Rudy Rogers, FBI agent Homer Southard, and a host of backup people were in Savannah within two hours of the discovery of Eddie Britain's car parked behind the late Ms. Pratt's modest home. Jerry Swanson was kept informed at his beach home in Edisto. No clues were found leading to Eddie's whereabouts. The local papers were flooded with pictures of Eddie and rewards were offered for any information.

The car was impounded and diligently searched inside and out. The boys in the lab got lucky with the trunk. Several strands of hair were found to be a DNA match for the hair of Liz Swanson. No body fluids or any indication of death came from the trunk. The odds seemed to say that she was still alive. At least she was alive when she was in the trunk. They hoped that Eddie had not disposed of her on the way to Savannah.

Once the search hit the street complete with a posted reward, a host of pretenders came forward looking for a fast buck. Most were quickly dismissed after a few questions. Mr. Don Kochi, however, was a different story. He was a local drunk who claimed to have seen Eddie shortly before the presumed murder. He pinpointed where he took Eddie and where he was dropped off. After questioning him about Eddie's appearance and mannerisms it was apparent that his story was legit. Mr. Kochi was thoroughly interviewed and rewarded with beer money.

Most likely Liz was not with him when he arrived in Savannah. It was also evident that Eddie went to see Ms. Pratt to cop a fake ID. The usual places were checked, the bus and train station along with the local cab companies. So far, everything was coming back empty.

One lingering question was "Why Mary Lou Pratt?" He seemed to have come directly to Savannah looking exclusively for her. She must have had some information that Eddie needed. There was more to it than just a simple fake ID. Did he come here looking for Jennifer? Had she taken the money and split, possibly with the pick-up man? This possibility was gaining strength. He had come here looking for her.

On this likelihood they ran an extensive public search for any information about Jennifer. A small motel operator just out of town came forward and provided proof that she had indeed spent three nights at his establishment and she was with a man. The motel operator, seeing a still photo of Sidney taken when he picked up the ransom money, believed that he was the one traveling with Jennifer. Eddie had come here looking for them. But where did they go from here? Evidently Eddie had gotten some choice information from Mary Lou before he killed her.

The FBI offered large rewards for any confirmed information about the trio. No credible information came in.

The hunt was now moving from a regional to a national search. He could have gone anywhere from Savannah. The chance that Eddie was still hanging around the Savannah area was remote. They had to assume that Eddie knew Jennifer's new ID and he was in pursuit. Any murder of a young affluent white woman would have to be investigated no matter where it occurred in North America or maybe even the world. Their mugs were appearing on every law enforcement computer screen in the Western Hemisphere.

Eddie saw the article about the Pratt slut and his car that linked him to her. It was a small article in the B section of the Pensacola newspaper. He hoped that Sidney and Jennifer were too busy partying to notice it. They were.

CHAPTER 23

Jake Brown, CEO of Strand Private Eye and all-around nice guy, settled into a booth at the Beach Deli and ordered coffee and a butter biscuit from his favorite waitress.

He couldn't help but reflect on how his simple life had gotten so involved. "Be a private eye, make a few bucks," that was what he thought when he got into the business. He figured since he retired from his exciting career as a letter carrier that he would get bored with retirement. Maybe so, but he never bargained for this. His simple life was turned on end that fateful day when Liz Alton gave him a call. One thing remained constant however; Jill Arthur still had the prettiest darn legs in Myrtle Beach.

"There, there, darling," she said. "I know you've got so much on your mind."

"I'm not so sure you want to hear what's on my mind."

"You're probably right. I haven't seen your cop buddy lately. What's his name, Rudy?"

"Yeah. He's a busy man. I think he's counting the days until he can retire. He was not expecting anything like this. Nobody was, not in Myrtle Beach."

Jill sat down across from him. "I don't know why you say that. Nothing surprises me about this place. Seems like we have a trainload of wackos coming in here everyday. These clowns are capable of anything."

Jake supposed she was right. This town was not immune to the same crap that was spreading like a cancer everywhere else. The world has always been full of crazy people. Myrtle Beach was no exception.

"So how's your love life?" Jake asked her.

"Same old stuff. Just waiting for Mr. Right to walk through the door. Until then, I'm wearing myself out telling all these red necks, cowboys and golfers, 'I ain't interested.' Other than that it's wonderful. How about yours?"

"How about mine, good question," Jake thought. He was getting very involved with Sally. Sleeping together a couple nights a week will do that. The rest of the week they did their own thing. It wasn't the ideal situation, but neither wanted to give it up.

"It's been worse," Jake finally said. "I guess you could say I got a steady girl."

"Do I hear wedding bells?"

"No, you don't hear wedding bells. How about some more coffee?" he said, wanting to change the subject.

"You got it," she said as she went to get his coffee and wait on some other customers. The place was starting to fill up.

Jake drank the rest of his coffee, read the paper and slipped out the door.

Liz was amazed at the ingenuity and simple desires of Osa and Holmes Chamblin. Chamblin was their last name, at least as far as they were concerned. A friend had performed a marriage ceremony several years before. They were husband and wife even if no one else in South Carolina knew about it.

Liz was intrigued at the assortment of wild sprouts and vegetables that Osa would find for dinner. Holmes always managed to catch several nice Spot Tail fish, or Drum, as some people would call them. They were caught with a little fish that Holmes would catch in a trap. He called them Mud Minnows. Some of the minnows were almost big enough to eat. Anyway you look at it, those fish and veggies were mighty good cooked over the open fire.

Liz did what she could to help. Mostly she helped Osa with the cleaning and dinner. She was also picking up on what they could eat and what they could not. To her surprise and not without a little hesitation, Liz found out that snake was quite good. It went especially well with pussy willows.

Osa and Holmes treated Liz with the utmost respect and dignity. They figured she was a cultured lady. Just how cultured, they had no idea.

Evening time on the swamp was beautiful, especially the hours just before sundown. Liz, Osa and Holmes were enjoying just such an evening.

"You haven't said much since you've been here," Osa said. "Anything you want to tell us?"

Liz had been silent about her abduction situation. She did not know what kind of an arrangement Holmes had with Eddie. Eddie had something on Holmes. There was little doubt about that. It might be very dangerous to say too much. She needed to go slowly.

"Just, thank you for being so nice to me. It's been a while since anyone has done that. You have been more than gracious."

"No problem," Osa said as she studied Liz. "You come from money don't you, honey?"

"Most of my life I've been a wealthy woman. I married well."

"Figured as much. There was just something about you. So what's your story?" Osa asked not really expecting an answer.

Liz had always prided herself in being able to judge people. These people were linked to Eddie somehow but they were genuinely good people. That fact was rather obvious. What choice did she have but to trust them? Trust was something she had naively taken for granted, but now, during these last several months, it had been ripped away. As in so many other areas of her life, in this too she felt like she had been violated. Despite her hurt, she had to trust them.

"My name is Liz Swanson. It used to be Liz Alton. My deceased husband's family owned Alton Mills." She noticed the surprise on their faces when she said that. "My husband, Harold Alton, passed away several years ago. I moved to Myrtle Beach after I sold my interest in the mill. I married Jerry Swanson the first of this year. Six months ago I was abducted near my home by Eddie Britain. He and his girlfriend held me captive in a dog lot. They abused me almost every night. If it wasn't for my faith, I don't think I could have survived."

By the expression on their faces Liz could not determine if they believed her or not. Undaunted, she continued.

"They contacted my husband and demanded a ransom. They got the money and somehow managed to escape. They had a helper. Some guy named Sidney. The girl took off with him and the money. As far as I can figure it, Eddie brought me here so he can go after them. I figure he will kill them if he finds them. When he's done with them, he will come back and get me. I'm sure he will kill me when he comes back. To tell you the truth, I'm not sure why he's let me live this long."

Liz finished her story and looked at Holmes and Osa. She was so anxious she could hardly breathe. What would they say?

"You's talkin bout Alton Mills? You's Ms. Lizzy of Alton Mills?" Holmes asked.

"That's me."

"So you're wanted by the police. I bet the whole world is looking for you," Osa said. "Oh, God. This is not good."

Osa and Holmes stood there with their mouths open. "You knew nothing about this?" Osa asked Holmes. He shook his head no. The concept of lying was foreign to Holmes.

"I suppose you want us to take you home?" Osa asked. "Well, we can't take you home. There are plenty of good old boys that want to string my man up. The very least he gets is life in prison. We can't take you out of here. I'm sorry."

"Whatever you've done, I'm sure I can help clear things up," Liz said. "I know most of the judges and all the top lawyers."

Holding up her hand, Osa continued. "Let me explain it to you, Liz. My man was accused, tried, and convicted of raping and killing a white woman in this county eighteen years ago. A lot of people were looking forward to seeing him hang. But Holmes managed to escape. We planned it and here we are. He shows his face anywhere again, he will not have a chance. Do you understand? This ain't no ivory tower world we're living in. This is the real south. Eighteen years ago poor blacks had no justice in Georgetown and it's not any better now."

"I can't imagine Holmes ever doing anything like that," Liz said.

"That's because he never did do it. He was set up. Somebody had to take a fall. He happened to be in the wrong place at the wrong time. Made things real convenient for the law enforcement community. Know what I mean? Don't even need facts, witnesses, or anything like that. Just another black man, string him up. Everybody goes home happy."

"How did he escape?"

"He was working on a road gang on a stretch south of town. There were about fifteen prisoners stretched out over about 150 yards. They had been working the same stretch every Thursday for about two months. One guard was at one end and the other guard at the other end. The woods were thick in that stretch. They didn't have any dogs."

Osa was noticeably upset but she continued. "Whenever I came in on Sundays to see Holmes, one of the guards always came on to me. He always managed to say something filthy to me. I didn't pay him any mind. Holmes figured maybe I could lure him into the swamp long enough for him to escape. I didn't want to do it but I didn't want my man to die either. Bottom line was I started flirting with him a little when I came to see Holmes. That old white man was going crazy.

"We had it planned. I came out of the woods one day near a thicket. I gave the horny guard the 'come on' and I started walking back into the woods. The fool followed me. When he had gone into the woods about forty yards, Holmes took off in the opposite direction. The other guard who was over 100 yards away managed to fire a couple shots at Holmes but it was too late.

"When the guard who was wanting me heard the shots he turned around and ran back to the road. By this time Holmes was gone. Those guys were no match for Holmes in the woods. I took off running the other direction and we met up at a place we planned. Anyway, we ended up out here in the swamp. We've been here ever since."

"My goodness. Surely there must be a way to prove his innocence?"

"I'm afraid that justice isn't in the cards for us."

"If he was proven innocent we could walk out of here," Liz said.

"We can't help you, Liz. I'm sorry. We can't take that chance. Our life is good here. We love our simple life. It ain't much to most people but to us everyday is a gift from God."

Liz could certainly understand that. Not a day went by that she did not thank God for this place and for another day of deliverance from Eddie.

What to do now was another question. She wanted to go home so desperately. She also knew she could never bring herself to betray these dear people.

"I don't know what's going to happen," Liz said, "but I know I will never betray the kindness that you have shown me. I'm new with this walking by faith stuff but I believe that God is going to work this out somehow. And when he does, it's going to be shouting time."

"Amen to that, sister, amen to that," Osa said as she gave Liz a warm embrace and whispered in her ear, "We won't let him hurt you, honey. I promise."

~

The sound of a couple of irate tourists next door woke Eddie up. She was complaining because he was in such a hurry and he was upset because she took all day to put her makeup on. After enduring several minutes of this heated dialogue, Eddie crawled out of bed.

Today he needed to find some work. Walking down the street he noticed that every other block on the beach had either a construction or a paint job going on. Eddie opted for a painting job. A particular crew called "Outlaw Paint" caught his eye. Compared to the rest of the crew, Eddie, or Mike as they called him, was down right clean cut.

Eddie worked all day everyday and hit several of the local dives each night. Ed and June Jones were nowhere to be found. After several weeks of work he managed to buy an old car.

He scanned the paper daily looking for the latest news on the case. With each passing week the articles were fewer and farther between. The press was becoming disinterested. No news was definitely good news.

He was going to lunch with his crew when he saw her cross the street in front of the car he was in. She was the same size as Jennifer but a blond instead of a brunette. Those tight leather pants were what tipped him off. Few women anywhere had a set of legs like Jennifer. She quickly disappeared into a row of shops.

"Stop the car! I need to get out. I'll see you guys at the job," he said as he darted out of the car. He decided to wait outside rather than follow her in. Most likely she would come out the way she went in. He grabbed a newspaper and took a seat on a park bench and waited. From his location he could either see her come out the way she went in, or he could see her come out the back way by the marina. He waited.

She appeared at the back by the marina. She stood and talked to a security guard for a moment and with a wave headed up the walk directly toward Eddie. It was her there was no doubt about it. Wearing the same expression she always wore, she was hot stuff and she knew it. She glanced his way for a moment but did not recognize him. Walking across the street she got into a red Jaguar convertible, license plate, number LZY-2017. Eddie jotted it down as she drove off heading toward the condos to the east. Eddie smiled and went looking for a hamburger and a beer.

CHAPTER 24

After three weeks in Edisto with no news about Liz, Jerry Swanson returned to Myrtle Beach. It had been four months since Liz had disappeared. It seemed like four years. Many of his friends had tried to encourage him to go on with his life. He knew with every passing day the chance of Liz being alive diminished. His friends hoped that he could begin to come to grips with the fact he may never see Liz again. Some were prompting him to get back into the political fray. He could not.

He had been a driven man for most of his adult life. Like most driven men he had met with considerable success. Since Liz's disappearance, however, he felt completely drained. Everything he did he forced himself to do. He knew he had to push himself because anything was better than the personal torment he had been through these past four months. Life had to go on.

Being a handsome, wealthy, and prominent man brought him frequent romantic opportunities. Now was not the time to wander down any of those paths. Would it ever be the time for another woman in his life? It was not a subject he cared to think about.

Linda was worth her weight in gold. She never missed a day and always kept things in perfect order. Many times when Jerry was at his wit's end, there was Linda with her calming, confident way, bringing peace out of turmoil.

"You didn't have to hurry back from the beach. I can handle this place," Linda said as she joined him at the dinning room table for a cup of her freshly ground gourmet coffee.

"A whole lot better than I do, I'm afraid."

"You've had more on you than any ten people should have to bear. I really don't know how you've done it. You're stronger than you think."

"Anyway, I really appreciate all you've done for us." Just saying the word "us" reminded him of his constant heartache since Liz's disappearance. Linda noticed the moisture forming in her boss's eyes.

"Mr. Southard called. He said they were widening the search."

"He's not coming by, is he?" Jerry asked.

"He didn't say he was."

"Let's hope not."

Even a sweet girl like Linda had a few people she would just as soon not see. Homer Southard, FBI agent and all around jerk, was one such person.

They sat in silence enjoying each other's company and the rich coffee.

"You'd be proud of me, Linda. I've been doing some praying lately. Haven't done any of that since I was a kid. I think it is helping."

"Prayer always helps. God has carried me all these years. I can't help but think that God is going to work this thing out for the good. I have no idea how. That's His business."

They sat in silence and watched the various birds at the feeders outside. In better days, Liz and Jerry would get excited whenever they saw a new specie at the feeder. Everywhere he looked he was reminded of Liz.

"The Bible says that God even knows when each one of those little sparrows falls to the ground. I know that He's watching over Liz."

"I hope so, Linda."

"No hope so about it, Mr. Swanson. Amazing thing is, He's watching over you, too."

"Now that is amazing," he thought. "It's easy to believe that God is watching over someone else. But watching over me? Now, that is a stretch." Still, he had to admire Linda's faith. It certainly had been a comfort. There was no denying that.

"Do you think she is still alive, Linda?"

She did not answer right away. She chose her words carefully. "I've thought a lot about it. I guess, logically, it does not look good. But I don't know. I've got this gut feeling that she's alive." She turned and looked at Jerry. "I believe she is going to come home. That's what I believe."

"I'm with you," Jerry winked. "I'm with you."

Holmes recounted his story again. He knew the woman who was murdered and raped, but he said he was not there when it happened. She was a wealthy banker's wife in her late thirties. Holmes was going to see her that day to do some yard work. She had him digging and moving some rocks. Holmes said she was always nice to him and never acted inappropriately in any way.

Shortly before Holmes arrived someone raped and killed Mrs. Thompson. A Mr. Ned Neely arrived a few minutes before Holmes got there. Neely was a local veterinarian. He was coming to look at the Thompson's mare. Finding her front door opened, Neely called out several times. There was no answer. Stepping inside, he saw the terrible scene. She lay dead on the living room floor.

Not five minutes later Holmes showed up at the door. He was a young black man, bulging with muscles and sweating from his five-mile walk. He would have been a prime suspect except Neely had seen him a few minutes before walking toward the Thompson home. Neely knew that Holmes couldn't have done it.

Ned Neely called the police. Holmes had to stay at the scene. When the police arrived and heard the story of how Mrs. Thompson was found, Holmes seemed more like a suspect every minute. Before the day was out they were sure they had the murderer. Holmes Chamblin did not have a chance. The all white jury deliberated less than thirty minutes. They found him guilty of first degree murder and rape.

"Why didn't Neely tell them that he saw you heading toward the house?" Liz asked. "You could not have been there when it happened."

"Gess dey jis founds it easy to blames me."

"Neely knew that he would be a suspect, too. It was so convenient to pin it on my man," Osa said. "And I guarantee you that the Klan, which I know had influence with the police, was behind the whole thing. That's exactly what happened."

"Do you think Neely did it?" Liz asked.

"No, I don't think he did. Everybody wanted a quick fix and in walks my man. All them good churchgoers were more than happy to lynch my man, more than happy. They were down right ecstatic about it."

"So you and Holmes have been a pair for a while."

"He's always been my love. Ever since I was twelve years old when I first laid my eyes on that sixteen-year-old hunk of muscle. You might say it was love at first sight. We have been together since right before all this mess started. I wasn't going to let him die in prison. We came up with a plan, he escaped and here we are."

"Is Neely still around?"

"Oh, yeah," Osa said, "He's still got his shingle hanging out. I doubt if he ever gives Holmes a second thought. I'm sure he thinks he's dead. He's a good church boy who's been playing around with some young black girls for years. I'm sure his wife doesn't have a clue. He frequents one of those houses that rich white men like so well. You know what I mean, all the love money can buy."

"Has anyone ever questioned him about his story?"

"Not that I know of. It wouldn't do any good. They would just keep coming up with more lies about Holmes. Like I say, they were ecstatic. I guess it brought back old memories for some of the good old boys. You'd think they just won the lottery, another black to hang."

"So you came with Holmes to live here?"

"He's my man for better or worse. And with him, it's always been for the better. My home will always be where he's at. I can't imagine many people happier than we are."

Liz couldn't imagine many either. From someone who knew what riches could buy, what they had money couldn't touch. She had to agree with Osa.

"I guess having a conscience attack would be out of the question for Neely?"

Osa laughed, "Yes, I think so."

"You think he could be bought, paid off for telling the truth, for crying out loud?" Liz asked.

"I'm sure he could be bought. I just don't think these gator skins are going to mean much to him. Now if we could throw in a few snakes, now that might be something else."

"Wats you's talk'n 'bout, missy?" Holmes asked.

"I'm a wealthy lady. I could pay him to tell the truth."

They looked at Liz with amazement. "So what are you thinking?" Osa asked.

"I'm thinking we make a contact with someone we can trust. Have them approach Neely. Offer to reward him handsomely if he comes clean about the facts. We get a radio and wait to hear it on the news. When we find out it's a done deal we walk out of here. You go free and I go home."

They sat in stunned silence. It just might work. From Liz's viewpoint it was all upside. From Holmes and Osa's it was a bit risky. It could backfire. It might not do anymore than stir up long forgotten anger and make things that much worse. There was always the possibility that Neely couldn't be bought, be it ever so remote. But if Neely did talk and Holmes was cleared that would be another story.

Eddie was certainly another factor to be considered. He could show up at anytime. It was possible that he would wait till Christmas to meet Holmes. If he got desperate he could come looking before Christmas. Eddie Britain would have no qualms about killing all three of them.

"I think it could work. We need to pray about it and sleep on it. One thing I don't want to see happen is for Eddie to show up here. That I don't want," Liz said.

"You have any ideas about a contact person?" Osa asked.

"I have someone in mind. He's a private eye in Myrtle Beach, a nice man that I trust completely. Let's sleep on this and talk some more tomorrow."

A glimmer of hope began to fill their hearts. Liz committed it to God and slept like a baby.

CHAPTER 25

Eddie spent his days painting and his evenings exploring the condo areas east of Pensacola Beach. He had not seen the red Jaguar that Jennifer had driven off in but it was only a matter of time.

It was late November and Eddie's life as Mike Helms was going smoothly. He was working on a good tan and hitting on a couple of the local beauties. He continued his nightly search for Jennifer and Sidney. She quite possibly had dumped that loser by now. The only thing that would possibly hold them together was the money. For Sidney's sake he had better be gone, better penniless than dead.

Six weeks after he first spotted Jennifer, Eddie hit pay dirt. Sticking out like a sore thumb at the Sea Manor Estates complex was a red Jaguar convertible license number LZY-2017.

The place was very upscale and had a security guard to keep nonresidents out. From what Eddie could tell he wasn't doing his job very well. People came and went as they pleased. The building had eleven stories and every room had a view of the Gulf.

Eddie parked his car and walked toward the tennis court and past her car to get a good look. There was nothing helpful inside, like a piece of mail with an address on it. He hung around a few minutes then left. He would try again tomorrow.

He followed the same routine every day for a week. On the seventh day he found what he was looking for. A magazine on the passenger side seat was addressed to June Jones, 716 Sea Manor Estates.

Now knowing the apartment number, Eddie spent some time hanging around the tennis courts and keeping an eye out for Sidney. He didn't have to wait long. He was getting ready to leave for the day when Sidney pulled into the lot driving a new Porsche and parked two cars down from Eddie.

With him was a young girl wearing a micro mini skirt. They hurried into the building. Sixty-five minutes later they emerged. They drove off and Sid returned by himself twenty-five minutes later. Sidney evidently had an afternoon appointment with a working girl. The thought of Sid flipping away his money infuriated Eddie. Sid's time was drawing nigh.

Eddie observed their schedules for five days. They were in and out a lot usually going their separate ways. There seemed to be one common denominator, they were never home for lunch. They were gone every day from eleven-fifteen till after one. This was the window of opportunity that Eddie was looking for.

The first Wednesday in December Eddie made his move. He parked his car in the back of the lot around 10 in the morning. Sidney left first at five till eleven. Jennifer was ten minutes behind him. Eddie walked in the door with a group of people and went to the elevator. Three people got on with him. Luckily no one else punched the seventh floor.

The hallway was empty as he made his way to 716. The door was locked. He began to shimmy it with a device that he used when he was working maintenance at Chesterfield. Perspiration formed on his forehead as he carefully worked the device. After three tries it worked and he stepped inside.

He took a few moments to scope out the place. It was impressive. "They must have bought it furnished," he thought to himself. Interior decorating was not what Jennifer did best.

He helped himself to a beer and settled into a chair around the corner from the door. Where he sat was out of sight from anyone who might come in.

His plan was simple. If Sidney came home first he would kill him on sight. His nine-millimeter pistol, complete with a silencer, was at his side. If he had a gal with him it would not be her lucky day. If Jennifer came in first, she would have a close encounter with duct tape. Nothing to do now but wait.

At 1:25 a key jingled in the door. Eddie stood quickly with his gun drawn waiting at the edge of the door. Sidney walked in and went quickly to the refrigerator. He grabbed a beer, threw his keys on the table and sipped his brew as he stood looking out the window toward the Gulf.

His back was to Eddie. His second sip of beer was his last as Eddie exploded a shell through his heart leaving a small hole in the sliding glass door that was now spattered with blood. Sidney fell to the floor like a sack of flour never knowing what hit him. A few spasmodic jerks and a slaughterhouse gurgle and Sidney was finished.

Eddie dragged him into the bedroom where he had been hiding and covered the blood on the carpet up with a throw rug. Jennifer could be home at any time.

Eddie sat and waited. After two hours went by, he started watching the main road from the balcony. It was the only road that approached the complex. Four hours and seven beers later, Eddie saw the Jaguar pull in. He waited in the same place he had waited for Sidney.

"Open the door, my hands are full. Sid, open the damn door!" she said impatiently.

Eddie gripped the pistol and opened the door in such a way that it shielded him from her. She stormed into the condo holding three bags of groceries.

"It's about time, fool. What took you so long?" she said as she sat the groceries on the kitchen counter.

"Hello, doll," was all he needed to say.

She froze as the breath went from her lungs, still not turning to face him.

"You look good in leather, especially in that hot Jaguar. I could have sworn I saw you a few weeks ago down at the Marina. Can you imagine how lucky we are. Two old lovers running into each other this way. Damn, you look good!"

"Sidney could be coming home soon," she managed to choke out still not facing him.

"I wouldn't worry about Sid if I was you. He's been here all afternoon. Turn around here, baby. Let me look at you."

She turned to face Eddie. Her color was completely gone. The gun's stock was bulging from his pocket.

"What happened to Sidney?"

"He had an unfortunate accident. It was pitiful. He was showing me how to handle a firearm and the boy shot himself right through the heart. It was downright awful. It was all I could do to get the blood up. He's in the bedroom if you need to see him.

"That was a pretty lousy deal you pulled back at the beach," Eddie said void of any emotion. "You had to know I'd come after you. We could have got away with it. We really could have. And here you went and messed it up."

"We could still get away with it," she said desperately. "We could. I still got most of the money. We could take off. Nobody would ever know. Just like old times."

"Wow, just like old times. I like that."

She started to approach him.

"I wouldn't do that, doll. I get real nervous when I have a gun. You don't want to see another accident do you?"

She shook her head no.

"Where is the money?"

"In a safe deposit box."

"What bank?"

"Sun Coast."

"What street is it on?"

"I, ah, I can't remember."

"Can't remember where five million dollars is? You must be working too hard. What's the box number?"

"I can't remember."

"Where's the key?"

"Damn it, Eddie. I can't remember."

He grabbed her by the back of her head and cupped her mouth shut. "Shut your damn mouth or I will kill you right now," he growled. "Do you understand me?"

She nodded her head yes.

"You got the money in here somewhere. Don't lie to me. I'm going to ask you one more time, where is the money?"

By now she could hardly breathe. Her heart was beating so fast she thought she would faint.

"I'll get it for you, Eddie. I will. Just please don't kill me. Please, Eddie. I don't want to die."

"Get me the money."

She hurried across the room to a desk that had a trick sliding top on it. Inside was a briefcase containing the money. She sat it in front of Eddie.

"How much have you and loser blown?"

"I don't know. We paid for this place. We each bought cars. I don't know. About seven hundred thousand dollars, I guess. Yeah, something like that."

"Leaving all that money here is dangerous. The police will figure that's what got Sid killed. Nasty wound, right through the heart," he smiled as only a cold-blooded killer could.

Eddie rose and walked toward the window. "I can't believe you did me like you did. It took the wind out of my sails. Sure did." He turned toward her. "Why'd you do it, baby?" She had no answer. He looked her hard in the eyes. "You think I'm going to kill you?"

She gasped, "No Eddie, you wouldn't kill me. We been through too much, you and me. We're a team."

"We used to be a team, bitch. Ain't no going back now. The way I see it, we got some problems here. We got a dead body in the other room. We got a pile of money that you stole from me. And we got to figure out what to do with you."

He walked to the window again, "Great view, very nice. I tell you what I'm going to do. I'm going to let you live. I'm even going to leave you some money. You were in on it from the beginning and it was as much your idea as mine. You get to stay here and explain to the police how you found Sidney lying on the floor, the poor bastard. One of the party animals that hangs around here must have come after him. Who knows. I'll leave the details to you."

"Thanks Eddie. I mean it, thanks. How much can you leave me?"

"A million. That will leave me a little over three. I imagine I can find me a new woman with that kind of money."

He counted out a million dollars and headed for the door. He turned and said, "Just call the police. Tell them that he has been killed. There is nothing here to link you to it. Just stay cool. You'll come out of this fine. Goodbye, Jennifer."

"Bye."

Eddie left and Jennifer called the police. Eddie stayed around town a couple of days just to hear the news about Sidney. There was not a lot to report. It was an apparent robbery attempt. Somebody thought they saw a suspicious looking hippie type hanging around. Jennifer was not a suspect. Maybe her luck was changing.

Eddie hung around town long enough to buy a new car and then headed toward Georgetown, South Carolina.

Driving up I-85 Eddie wished that he had just done away with Liz Swanson. He would have except he was not sure if he could find Jennifer and Sidney. If he could not find them he needed her for leverage. She was the one person who could put the finger on Jennifer if she didn't want to come across with the cash.

That matter settled, the rich broad needed to be dealt with. Finding her would be the trick. Eddie figured he would look for information as to Holmes's whereabouts in the swamp. If he didn't get a lead he would wait around until Christmas when Holmes was expected to come into town.

He didn't like the idea of hanging around Georgetown for three weeks. He did not like that at all. Liz had been a well-known person in Georgetown for many years. There were reports of huge sums of money offered to anyone that could lead the authorities to him. Anything could happen. He would not take any chances.

Since he had the cash and a new ID, he had given some thought to just forgetting the girl. Let Holmes enjoy his white woman in the swamp. "I'm sure he ain't complaining," Eddie thought. He wrongly assumed that Holmes had as little class as he did.

Eddie wanted to put an end to this whole thing. He had said goodbye to Jennifer and Sidney. Now it was time to finish off Liz. Finish her off and the page is turned. Everything from his past would be gone. Goodbye Eddie Britain, hello Mike Helms.

CHAPTER 26

On a chilly December morning, Liz and Osa worked on the letter to be sent to Jake Brown, 108 Palmer Street, Myrtle Beach. After some discussion they came up with a letter:

Dear Jake,

I need your help. There are many details that I must leave out which I hope to give you at the proper time. I am safe for the moment but continue to be in a potentially dangerous situation. Time is of the essence in this matter. Because of increased danger to my new acquaintances and myself, you must promise not to tell anyone about this message, including the police or my husband. Our safety and yours cannot be compromised.

We have derived a plan for my escape from my present dangerous situation. It is dependent upon the success of this plan. If it is not successful then I tried and I thank you for your effort.

Eighteen years ago, a black man in Georgetown was accused of raping and murdering a banker's wife named Edna Thompson. The black man's name is Holmes Chamblin. He was convicted on the testimony of Mr. Ned Neely, a Georgetown veterinarian. The police were anxious for a conviction and were more than happy to frame Holmes for the murder. Holmes later escaped while awaiting execution.

I want you to find Ned Neely and offer him five million dollars to tell the truth about what actually happened that day. After he gives his truthful statement about Holmes, the money will be delivered to him at the statue at River Park. Another party will deliver the money.

The truth is what we want. The truth is not what he testified to at the trial. He will be reprimanded for not telling the truth, but he will not do jail time. Have him check with a lawyer, but I know that will be the case.

The truth will be that Holmes Chamblin could not have murdered Mrs. Thompson because he was walking toward her house a mile or so away when Neely passed him on the road. Neely then went to her house and found Mrs. Thompson dead. Holmes walked in several minutes later. Holmes could not have done it.

When you hear Mr. Neely give this account in front of the district attorney, instruct him to go to the statue at the River Park at exactly noon. There will be a man there. Mr. Neely is to say to the man, "Lovely day, isn't it?" This will be the cue for the man to hand over the money. You must not under any circumstances follow him to the park or in any way observe the transaction. Doing so would put my acquaintances and myself in grave danger. Mr. Neely is to take the money and leave the park immediately.

If he won't talk, threaten him with your knowledge of a certain house on James Street, a house full of young black girls, some of them not thirteen years old. Tell him we have the contacts to implicate him. If he talks, we will forget the whole nasty business.

If he agrees and testifies, this will be a major news item in Georgetown. It will be in the newspapers and on the radios. If it is successful, I will meet you at the River Park in Georgetown at 9 p.m. on Christmas Eve. If it doesn't work, I may not get out of this alive.

Pray that this works. Remember, you must not tell anyone. This is crucial!

The day before the testimony, place an ad in the Savannah paper in the personal section. Simply say, "Tomorrow is the day." This will assure the delivery of the money.

Your friend,

Liz Swanson

Later that evening, Holmes left with the letter to Jake and also a letter to Jerry addressed to his private mailbox. He would spend the night in the woods near a paved road about 300 yards behind a small dusty store. The following morning he would drop off the letters and purchase a small transistor radio. His trip was successful and he arrived back in camp the following evening. All they could do now was wait.

~

"And I'm telling you that you can eat the damn things. When you fry 'em up, you can't even tell they got that bag. You're a puss. That's your problem." Joe Lane said.

Joe was a cranky old slob on the best of days. This was not one of his better days. Doc James had told him earlier in the day that he needed to start taking medicine for diabetes and Joe wasn't happy.

Joe was talking about a blowfish that he had caught from the pier. He was sure they were edible. Of course, it would be a cold day in you know where before he actually ate one.

"I tell you what, Joe, take them home with you and let me know how they taste. I'm sure Jane can make them edible."

"Gutless. That's your problem," Joe said.

When Jake was in Joe's company, he couldn't help but ask himself, "Why am I here?" He concluded that he must have a psychological disorder. Why else would he choose friends like Joe?

The regular pier rats preferred this time of year on the pier. They might gripe and moan because there were no young women around. If the truth were known, they liked the solitude brought about by the cool fall weather. Young women for these guys were only a memory anyway.

Jake hadn't worked his way up to what was considered a regular rat yet. Worked his way down, might be a better way of putting it. Anyway there was something relaxing about not catching anything on an almost vacant pier.

Fourteen months had passed since Liz Swanson first called Jake and six months had passed since she had been abducted. It seemed longer than that. There was probably a better chance of pulling a ten-pound flounder out of these cold waters than of her still being alive.

He thought about visiting Jerry Swanson but what could he say? What could anyone say? Why bad things happening to good people had always been a question with no easy answer. People have often asked, "How could a good God allow this to happen?" "It's a fallen world" had always been the answer that most readily came to mind. "Life can be very unfair," Jake mused as he stared across the ocean, "very unfair indeed."

"I've eaten these things all my life. It's idiots like you who never want to try anything new. You have heard of color TV, haven't you?" Joe barked.

"I'm sorry. Did you say something intelligent?" Jake countered trying to get on Joe's level.

Joe gave Jake one of those stares that said either, "I'm going to kill you" or "I'm crazy, leave me alone." It was hard to tell which one it was.

Seeing that this conversation was going nowhere fast, he tipped his hat to Joe, and walked off of the pier. And to think he had actually looked forward to retirement for the past twenty years. Life rarely ends up the way you figure it. On the way out he called Sally about a dinner date, got a cup of coffee for the road and headed for home.

∼

Jake read the letter for the third time. He sat down in his easy chair and patted his dog's head. He looked through his filing cabinet and pulled out all the correspondence he had ever received from Liz. Even to his untrained eye the writing was a perfect match. Liz was alive and he couldn't tell a soul. He could not for the life of him figure out why. He had to take her word for it. She was trusting him with her life.

His evening with Sally was uneventful. They grilled chicken and drank a beer or two. She had some things to do at home so she couldn't spend the night. "Just as well," Jake thought.

After bacon and eggs the next morning and his second cup of coffee, Jake headed for Georgetown.

∼

Jerry Swanson was a creature of habit. One of the things he always did was make his seven-mile trip to check his private mailbox twice a week. Most of the time the mail was something from a special interest group looking for a political favor or maybe a credit card application.

When he saw the letter his heart stopped. It looked like Liz's handwriting. He left hurriedly and opened the letter in his car.

My Dear Jerry,

   I love you.

   I am still in grave danger. I have a plan of escape and I need you to help. You will have many questions when you read this letter. I wish I could answer them all, but I cannot now. You just need to trust me on this and do what I say. Above all, do not tell anyone about this letter or what it entails. Our safety and yours depends upon it.

   When you see an ad in the personal section of the Savannah paper that says, "Tomorrow is the day," withdraw five million from our account. The following day take the money to the statue at the River Park in Georgetown. Be there by noon. A man will approach you and say, 'Lovely day isn't it?' Give the money to him. No questions asked.

   This will trigger a chain of events that, if all goes well, will result in my meeting you at the statue at River Park on Christmas Eve at 9 p.m. I can't explain how it will happen. You must just trust me that it could.

   If this does not work, I will not be there. I may not even be alive.

   Regardless of the outcome, you have been and will always be the love of my life. Not a day has gone by that I have not wept at the thought of what you must be going through.

   It is crucial for my safety that you do not share this information with anyone, even if I fail to arrive on Christmas Eve.

   As terrible as this ordeal has been, it has only strengthened my love for you and my thankfulness to God for bringing us together.

   Love always and forever,

   Liz

~

Ned Neely lived an uneventful but comfortable life in Georgetown. His veterinarian practice had been a fixture in town for twenty-five years. He and his wife May had three children, two sons and a daughter. All three were grown and had achieved a level of success in this part of the south, meaning they were not dead or in jail. His wife sang in the choir and he was at First Baptist every Sunday nodding his approval from his personal pew. Life was reasonably good for Ned Neely.

The matter about the Chamblin case was water under the bridge as far as Ned was concerned. It had been years since his conscience had given him even the slightest nudge of guilt. He had always figured that Holmes had probably done something worthy of death anyway. Bottom line was, nobody really much cared what happened to him. At least that's how Ned and his running buddies felt.

Ned Neely had it pretty good. Of course it would be nice to have a little more money. The house was paid for, and he still owed a little on the kids college. His retirement was coming up in a few years and they had enough to squeak by, more than some but not as much as others. Ned had dabbled some in the market. Like many people, by the time he got in the really great gains seemed to be past history. He was hoping that history would repeat itself.

His marriage was rather joyless. They married right out of high school. They had their kids and he finished vet school. Ned had always had an eye for the ladies. Early on his wife May had caught him in a compromising way with one of his employees and she threatened to leave him. It scared the crap out of Ned and he put on a good front for a while. Didn't last too long though. A friend turned him on to a place on the south side of town that had an abundance of young black girls who were willing for a price. Ned made it a point to carry a couple of hundred in pocket money which he emptied about twice a month.

"May I speak to Mr. Neely?" Jake asked a heavily made-up blond at the window of the veterinarian office.

"He doesn't see salesmen on Tuesdays," was her reply.

"I'm not a salesman. It is rather urgent."

She gave him that "yeah, I bet" look and disappeared around the corner. A few moments later Neely came to the window. He was a plain-looking man around fifty-five years old. He was thin, wore glasses and seemed to have reasonable intelligence. Jake handed him his private eye card.

"What is this all about?" Ned spewed. "I've got work to do and I ain't got time for your foolishness."

"I know, and I respect a working man. I just need thirty minutes of your time, maybe around lunchtime. Could you manage that?"

"I have no idea what this is about and I've got better things to do than waste my time with you. I'm a busy man, Mr., uh, Mr. Brown," he said reading the card.

"I know it's an inconvenience. I guarantee you that it will be in your best interest to meet with me. What time is your lunch?"

Ned was coming to the realization that maybe he should find out what this was all about. After all, Ned had more than a few skeletons in his closet.

"I'll meet you at Checks at 12:30. Thirty minutes is all you get," he said as he stuck the card in his pocket and headed for the back. The counter girl returned and gave Jake her "you can leave now" look. He obliged.

Checks was the kind of place that every southern town had. It was located on Highway 17 heading south just over the river. It was located in a building that should have been condemned twenty years ago. A gravel driveway surrounded the building. The place was full of free-standing tables and hungry eaters.

They met at the door and were directed to a smoking booth in the corner. After they both ordered the daily special, Ned lit his unfiltered cigarette and sipped his tea while looking at Jake with disdain.

"Talk to me. You've got thirty minutes."

"Tell me about Holmes Chamblin," Jake said noticing Neely's surprise.

"He's either dead or gone. I don't know which and tell you the truth, I don't much care."

"Somebody told me he wasn't guilty."

"Ask any black in town and that's exactly what they will tell you. Ask anyone else and you get a different story."

"What do you say about it, guilty or not guilty?"

"I believe this ground's been covered. He was tried and convicted a long time ago. It's history."

"Somebody told me there's a different story to be told. One that's a lot closer to the truth. Somebody told me you knew what that story was. I believe that you were the main witness, isn't that right? In fact, you were the only witness."

Neely crushed out his cigarette and glared across the table at Jake. "You can't believe everything you hear. I saw what I saw. You can read about it down at the courthouse. It's part of the public record. I ain't reciting it for no ten cent private eye."

"My client has instructed me to offer you money provided you come forward with the truth about what happened. They have informed me what they think the truth is. It's not exactly the version you recited in court."

"Are you saying I lied under oath?"

"I'm saying that my client says there is a different story and you know what it is. Recite it, and you cash in."

"If by some wild chance I did lie, just what is this 'client' of yours offering?"

"Upon your testimony before the district attorney of the truth concerning Holmes Chamblin which lines up with the truth as they have told me, you will receive five million dollars in cash."

Their food had arrived several minutes previous. When Jake mentioned the dollar amount, Neely sprayed a mouthful of fried squash across two tables. A sizeable hunk of squash landed on the forehead of a large, vicious looking southern belle who suddenly had murder on her mind. They ignored her seething stare. "What kind of joke is this?" Neely finally managed.

"Is the truth worth five million to you, Mr. Neely?"

"What kind of strange client do you have? Nobody cares that much about some damn loser like Holmes Chamblin," Ned said as he abruptly got up. "This is pure bull. That's what this is."

"Sit down cowboy. When was the last time you walked away from five million?"

He sat back down. "I've got a reputation in this town. People just don't lie in court. I can't just announce to everybody in town that I'm a liar. I don't give a crap what kind of money you're offering. Besides, what if my version of the truth doesn't line up with your client's so-called version?"

Jake wiped his chin with his napkin. "If your story doesn't line up, I guess you won't get paid. Like I say, tell the truth and you're going to cash in. About your reputation, I know how important that can be. It's perfectly understandable. I know some folks on James Street. They been telling me all about your good name."

Neely stared across the table with cold eyes, "Don't mess with me, boy. You mess with me and I'll screw you up big time."

"My client, who pays me very well, has given me instructions. I was told that you either come across with the truth and everybody is happy, or the little woman, not to mention the vice squad are going to be getting some news. They tell me that some of those girls down there are barely twelve years old? Tell me it ain't so, Ned?

"Tell me what your story is Neely. We need to get this ball rolling. The ball is going to roll. One way or the other, it is going to roll."

Neely was sweating profusely by this time. He knew he was playing with fire down at that whorehouse. He had been telling himself for years to let it go, but he just kept going back for more. The snake finally bit him.

"How do I know you're telling me the truth?" Neely asked.

"You don't know. You're going to have to trust me. Life can be that way sometimes."

Neely sat there immobilized as his mind raced. What could he do? He knew enough about the law to know he would not go to jail. He would have to endure some kind of counseling and he would be publicly humiliated. His wife, May, might leave him. "Not if she finds out about the money," he thought. With five million he could leave this backward town, go somewhere where nobody knew him, and retire in style. What did he have to lose?

He talked and Jake listened. His version lined up perfectly.

Chapter 27

Eddie headed into Georgetown with more than a little apprehension. He was known well enough to be recognized by dozens of people. Even though his new image was a sharp contrast to the old one, he wasn't planning on just hanging around in the open. He was now a wanted man with a hefty price on his head. Anybody he knew would cash him in without hesitation.

He found a room north of town near Pawleys Island. He could remain there without much chance of being noticed since about everyone there were tourists.

Rather than wait until Christmas for Holmes to show up he was inclined to try to find him now. The girl would be easier to dispose of in the swamp.

Eddie bought some beer and flirted with a couple of teenage girls in the next room. He might get lucky. He would check on Holmes tomorrow.

The next morning he woke up with his usual hangover. Fortunately he didn't drink all the beer. It seemed the young girls in the adjoining room had a taste for suds. The last one slipped out sometime before dawn. "Let's hope Mommy and Daddy don't find out," Eddie thought as he put on his pants and shirt and headed for the local egg shack for breakfast.

Eddie hung out around the motel most of the day with one brief excursion to the beach. He figured his best bet for finding out anything concerning Holmes was to head for the Roadhouse. Jamaul might be there and he definitely didn't want to run into him. He thought he would be okay. His hair was lighter and shorter and his mustache was gone. There was no point in going anytime before 10:30. He bided his time.

Eddie pulled into the parking lot at Abraham's Roadhouse about a quarter till eleven and was met by a highly intoxicated young black beauty who threw her arms around his neck as he stepped out of his car.

"I don't think this is a good idea," he said as he released her arms.

"Another time, darling. Another time," he said as he headed for the front door. One guaranteed way to get killed was to latch on to a black girl in a place like this, especially in the parking lot. The place was crowded. He headed for the bar and ordered a draft. The band was throbbing with a combination of funk and blues. This had to be the hottest place in Georgetown.

He correctly figured the best way to survive in a place like this was to mind your own business and try not to stick out. That was not easy. He was the only light-skinned person in the house.

There were at least 300 people inside and who knows how many in the parking lot. Eddie hung around until 12:30. He did not recognize anyone. He struck up a couple of conversations but wasn't able to steer either one toward the subject of Holmes Chamblin. He would try again tomorrow.

~

Neely spent a sleepless night with his mind going in a thousand different directions. Jake was to meet him at the courthouse at 9 in the morning. From there they were to proceed to the district attorney's office. At that time he was going to confess to lying under oath and obstruction of justice. What a happy day this promised to be.

The longer Ned thought about it the more ridiculous this all sounded. If it were not for the crap about the girls down on James Street he would tell Jake Brown to take a walk. For 95 percent of his life he was a model citizen. His one vice was threatening to do him in.

Ned was hoping that this had all been a bad joke. Just maybe Jake Brown would not be at the courthouse and Ned could go on with his life of undetected crime. He was not so lucky. As he approached the courthouse he spotted Jake feeding the pigeons what was left of a morning biscuit.

"And Mr. Neely, how are you this fine morning?"

"Not a good place to kill this worm," Ned thought as he stood next to the bench Jake was sitting on. "Peachy keen," he said.

"Are you ready to rumble?" Jake said trying to be cute. He was not succeeding.

"I'm ready to collect. That's what I'm ready to do."

"Now, now, first things first. We need to go see the man first. I say let's do it," Jake said as he got to his feet.

They entered the courthouse and were directed to the office of District Attorney Anthony Taylor who happened to be the first black public official ever elected in Georgetown. A local sports hero and minister, he had made friends on both sides of the track, black and white, rich and poor, men and women, especially women. He was a good-looking rascal.

"Mr. Neely. Don't tell me, I forgot to get my heart worm pills on my last visit. Am I right?" he said with a smile as wide as the room.

"No, I think you're up to speed there, Anthony. This is another matter I'm afraid."

Sensing the apprehension in Ned's voice, he motioned him to sit down. Looking at Jake he said, "And you are?"

"Jake Brown, Strand Private Eye. I work out of Myrtle Beach." With the look that Taylor gave him, Jake figured that one of the birds must have crapped on his bald head.

Obviously concerned, he offered Jake a seat. Concern was certainly a natural reaction when confronted with a private investigator, especially when you had something to hide. Anthony Taylor was a fine man but certainly there were a few things he would not want made public, a few indiscretions. But heck, the last one was more than a month ago. He felt clean as a newborn lamb. After all, you're only guilty if you're caught.

"Ned, what's this about?" he asked.

"I've got a matter I need to talk about. And I think I'm going to need this conversation recorded. Yeah, I think that would be a good idea," Ned said. The sweat was pouring off his head even though the room temperature was quite comfortable.

"Certainly," he said as he called for Ms. Lansing. If her skirt had been any shorter she would have been arrested. After she was situated Taylor motioned for Ned to go ahead.

Poor Ned recounted the details of how he and some of his buddies framed Holmes for the rape and murder of Mrs. Edna Thompson. He explained the pressure he was put under by the local authorities and how anxious they were to have a quick conviction. He stumbled and sweated his way along for a full forty minutes with the seductive Ms. Lansing recording every ugly word. When he finished he waited like a scalded dog for the whip to land.

"What the hell got in to you? What were you thinking?" was all that the respected minister and public servant could manage. He motioned the girl to leave and despite the intensity of the moment, they all watched her leave.

"I don't know what to say. I'm afraid it's the truth," Ned choked out.

"Mr. Chamblin has spent his whole adult life on the run. Who knows, he may even be dead," Taylor said with his best self-righteous voice as he strolled around the room. "How come we didn't hear about this years ago? How come you're talking now?"

"Some kind of choice," Ned thought. "Either jail for statutory rape or five million dollars. Hmm, that's a tough one." He continued, "I have no excuse. I really don't. I just couldn't keep it in me anymore. It was eating me up."

"This guy's a good liar," Jake observed.

"Your name is going to be mud in this town. You do know that? Business, church, you name it, you're finished Ned. All I can say is your conscience is in good working condition. Which leads me to wonder, what's he have to do with this?" he said pointing toward Jake.

"I needed the advice of someone who had some experience in such matters but was not part of the law enforcement community," Ned said.

"So you advised him to come clean, to throw everything away?"

"I always advise my clients to do the honorable thing," Jake said being proud of himself for lying almost as good as Ned. Almost was the operative word here.

"Throw everything away and come clean on something that will ruin his reputation and open up a whole new can of worms? I hope you didn't charge him too much for that counsel. If my lawyer gave me advice like that I would kill him. And if I was stupid enough to listen to it I would kill myself because I wouldn't be fit to live."

Neither Jake nor Ned said anything. They were obviously dealing with someone who had been around the block a few times.

"There's going to be some repercussions I can assure you of that. I'm not sure what at this time. I don't think you will go to jail. But to be honest with you, I don't hardly see how you're going to be able to hang around this town. If we don't put you in jail for a while, there's going to be plenty of people who will want some answers. You're not making my job any easier, I'll tell you that."

Anthony Taylor got up and gazed out the window. "Get out of here, Ned. Don't leave town. I will be in touch," he said with a strong emphasis on the "will" part.

Jake and Ned scurried out.

Ned left the courthouse sweating like a hog and smelling like one, too. They walked to the park bench where Jake had been feeding the birds earlier.

"I got some money coming, pus face," Ned said angrily. He gave Jake a look that said, "You don't have the guts to double cross me on this."

"Hey, I'm just the messenger. Your payday will be at noon and not a moment before. We got an hour and a half to kill. I guess we can feed the birds."

"Feed the birds if you want to, numb nuts. I'm getting me a cold one," Ned said as headed for the beer joint across the street. Normally he would be concerned about his Baptist buddies seeing him in a beer joint. It looked like Ned's days for caring were coming to a rapid end.

At ten till twelve when Ned stumbled out of the beer joint and met Jake at the bench next to the courthouse, he looked like anything but the respected Georgetown businessman. He could have passed as the village bum except that he was wearing a suit.

"It's payday, clown," Ned spewed out as he approached Jake.

"Yes, it is," Jake said. "Go to the River Park. There will be a man there next to the statue. Go up to him and say, 'Lovely day, isn't it?' He will give you the money. You take the money and walk away immediately, no questions asked. Do you understand?"

"What's not to understand? And what about you?"

"You will never see me again."

"But . . ."

"There ain't no buts about it. It's five till. You can walk there by noon.

Get going," Jake said as he turned and left Ned standing there.

"But what if the jerk isn't there? What if I don't get the cash?"

"You'll be able to sleep tonight with a clear conscience. Goodbye."

Ned hurried to the park. The park had a few people milling around looking for a little sanity in the middle of the workday. A young mother with a little boy was sitting on one side of the statue. On the other side stood a distinguished looking man who seemed quite fidgety. This had to be the guy.

Jerry Swanson saw Neely arrive at the park. Jerry thought Neely was a bum but he kept on stumbling toward him. Jerry wanted to ask him a million questions but he could not. He had to take Liz's word for the fact that this could bring her harm. He watched Neely approach until he was within an arm's length.

"Lovely day, isn't it?" the sweating Neely stated.

"Yes it is," Jerry Swanson said as he reluctantly handed away five million dollars for the second time in five months. Liz's safe return was priceless but this had to end.

Ned took the canvas satchel and quickly looked inside. It was filled with neatly bundled 100-dollar bills. "I guess honesty really is the best policy," he said as he smiled at Jerry Swanson.

Jerry did not smile back. Ned left the park in a hurry and headed home with his bag of loot. He had some explaining to do. The loot should make the explaining easier. There's nothing like cash to smooth the rough edges.

Jerry, still in a daze, headed back to Myrtle Beach.

CHAPTER 28

District Attorney Anthony Taylor called a press conference for one that afternoon. The local radio stations were notified along with both the TV stations. Taylor loved a crowd and he made the most of it.

He went on to describe the local news blockbuster. The event was carried live. The local veterinarian and city officials of days gone by sold Holmes Chamblin down the river and were more than happy to have Holmes meet his maker for something he didn't do. Of course he voiced his disdain for any kind of racism and he himself as District Attorney was living proof of the attitude change of the new south, and all the congregation said, "amen."

Fortunately for Ned, he managed to stutter the story to his wife May, complete with their unbelievable payoff, just in time for them to take their phone off the hook and pack their bags for a getaway to a local motel. Staying home was not a good option. They phoned Anthony Taylor and told him where they would be.

Listening in another world thirteen miles away as the crow flies, Liz, Osa, and Holmes heard the breaking story. Holmes and Osa hugged and cried and hugged and cried some more. For the first time in more than eighteen years they were free people, no longer needing to hide. They would leave for town in the morning. The plan was to spend one night at camp on the way and get into town the next day.

The prospect of leaving the swamp excited Liz, and yet she could not help but worry about Eddie. Where was he now? If he were in the area, these were going to be very tense times. He would either run or intensify his search for her. It all depended upon whether or not he had heard the news. There was no way of telling. She had to leave it in God's hands.

Later that evening, the three of them enjoyed the setting of the sun from a location where the surroundings hadn't changed in hundreds if not thousands of years. They relaxed, and yet there was a hint of uneasiness in the air.

Holmes spoke first. "I's jes don't know whats to think. I feel safe here. Dis is my home. I's got my woman."

No one could argue with what he said. He had peace here. In many ways this patch of swamp was heaven on earth. What would civilization bring to Holmes's world? He had little or no book knowledge but he had a world of horse sense. Liz knew that they would be fine. Holmes and Osa were people of true integrity in a world that was seriously lacking that very thing. They were two of the finest people she had ever known. Regardless of what happened they would have a special place in her heart for the rest of her life.

"We're going to have to go, baby," Osa said. "You're a good man. You will make me proud. Just like you've made me proud everyday we've been here. God has taken care of us, hasn't He? He always has and He always will."

They sat in silence as the evening sky became colored with shades of red and yellow. The swamp birds sang their evening song and the myriad of frogs brought forth their rhapsody. They were all deep in thought. The prospect of being home in two days seemed too good to be true. Since this nightmare began, nothing could be taken for granted. There were no more sure things. Things could change at any moment, depending upon the whereabouts of Eddie Britain.

"I can't help but think that he's out there," Liz said.

"I won't let him hurts you, missy. Holmes die first."

Liz hung her head and cried when Holmes said that. She knew it was true. This simple man would die for her. Holmes had only known her for three months and he would die for her. She realized at that moment she would die for them, too. Liz could not stop weeping. Osa gently held her hand as they silently contemplated their life to come.

Eddie spent the day lounging around the motel and pool. The news about Holmes had not yet reached him. He drank beer and slept most of the day away. His business that day would be in the evening. He was in for quite a shock.

He arrived at Abraham's Roadhouse around 10. The place had not filled up yet and Eddie was able to get a seat at the bar. After two hours of drinking Eddie struck up a conversation with a thirty-five-year-old man named Mitchell and joined him at his table.

Four men and two women were seated at the table. Mitchell introduced him to the table as Mike Helms. Eddie forgot the names as soon as he heard them. The table was into dancing and one of the girls at the table dragged Eddie onto the floor. They danced three or four sets before the band stopped and they headed back to the table. As they approached the table Eddie heard Mitchell say something about Holmes Chamblin to one of the girls at the table.

"What did you say about Holmes?" Eddie asked.

With that, Mitchell lit up and became very animated, "Man, ain't that something about Holmes?" he said with a huge grin.

"Ain't what something?"

"Man, you haven't heard? Holmes was cleared. A white veterinarian confessed to framing Holmes for that trumped-up murder charge. Holmes is a free man. I expect he'll be right here celebrating by this weekend."

Eddie felt a sudden wave of shock. "When did this happen?"

"Today. Brother Anthony Taylor, our district attorney, announced it at a press conference. He said anyone who might know of Holmes's whereabouts, should contact Holmes and tell him to come in. He is a free man."

"I guess he will be coming in around Christmas. Probably within a couple weeks," Eddie thought out loud.

"That's what I figure, if not sooner. If he has a radio, which I suspect he does, he could be coming in any day now. Yes sir, any day."

Eddie bought the table a round and left shortly thereafter. By this time, he was quite drunk. He managed to get to the motel without being stopped.

Back at the Roadhouse the night was winding down. Skoo got up from Mitchell's table and headed home. He couldn't shake the uneasy feeling he had about this Mike character. His intense interest in Holmes especially got Skoo's attention. He would talk to his mother in the morning.

Millie Stackpole was frying bacon and eggs to serve along with homemade biscuits and fresh apple butter. The coffee was brewed and ready to be served.

"Skoo honey, get up. Your breakfast is ready," she hollered to her son sleeping in the next room.

Several minutes later he came to the table and gave his mother a peck on the cheek as he passed by.

"Morning, Mamma."

"Morning, Son."

They enjoyed their breakfast and were working on their second cup of coffee.

"Mamma, somethins strange at the club lass night. Some honkey kept askin bout Holmes. He's been der befo. I remember. He was askin' bouts Holmes den, too. Name was Mike somethin. Mamma, he reminded me of dat Eddie boy up der at the beach that kidnapped Ms. Lizzy. You's got a picture, don't you?"

Millie Stackpole got up from the table and began looking through a drawer next to the sink. Shortly, she came back to the table with a newspaper picture of Eddie Britain. She laid it on the table in front of Skoo.

"Dat's him, Mamma. He's at the club las night. Dat him, ain't no doubt. He made himself blond. Goin' by da name of Mike, but dat's him. I's knows it, Mamma."

She got up from the table and again looked through the drawer. She located Jake Brown's business card and dialed his number.

"Hello," Jake answered on the second ring.

"Millie Stackpole, Mr. Jake. Down here in Georgetown."

"Yes, Millie, of course, what's up?"

She proceeded to tell Jake her son's account.

After getting off the phone with Millie, Jake took a deep breath and patted his dog Amos's head. What was he going to do? The letter Liz had written made it very clear that no one was to know of these developments. She specifically mentioned the police.

If Eddie was in Georgetown she could be in grave danger. Apparently Eddie did not know of Liz's whereabouts. That's assuming that Liz was hiding with Holmes, which seemed the most likely scenario. Despite what Liz said in the letter, they had to find Eddie. If Eddie finds Holmes then Liz is as good as dead. Jake dialed the number of the Myrtle Beach Police Department and asked for Rudy Rogers.

"Hey Jake, what's up?"

"I need to meet you at the Deli. It's important."

"I can be there in ten minutes."

"I'll see you there," Jake said as he hung up the phone and headed for town.

"Coffee for me, thanks," Rudy said to Jill.

"Same," Jake winked.

"This better be good. You interrupted my afternoon nap."

Jake proceeded to tell him everything that had transpired within the last few days, the letter from Liz, the dealings with Ned Neely, and the tip about Eddie Britain.

"Why didn't you tell me when you first received the letter from her?" Rudy demanded.

"I couldn't, Rudy. This girl for some misguided reason is trusting me with her life. She told me not to tell. Here's a copy of the letter," he said handing it to Rudy.

He studied the letter for a couple minutes, "And you think this is authentic?"

"It absolutely is. She wrote it."

Sticking it in his pocket he said, "I need to have this analyzed."

"She's has to be with Holmes, Rudy. Why else would she be concerned about clearing his name? She clears his name, and they walk out. They are probably walking out right now, and Britain is waiting and looking for them. We've got to find him before he finds them. He will kill her in a heartbeat. We don't have time to analyze this damn thing. We got to move and move now."

They left ten dollars on the table and hurried out.

Within two hours hundreds of police and sheriff deputies from Myrtle

Beach and surrounding areas descended on Georgetown. The FBI was an hour behind. Police were on every street checking every home and motel. The search was futile. Eddie was not in town. He was already in the swamp.

~

Liz, Holmes, and Osa left the camp at 10 in the morning. It was possible to make it to the road in one day but it would have been a hard day and it wasn't necessary. It would have been fine for Holmes but much too hard for Osa and Liz. Their plan was to get within two miles of the road and camp there. That would leave them with a four-hour trek to the road the next day.

Following Holmes's skilled leading, the threesome found a suitable campsite to spend the night. They built a small fire and settled in.

Eddie knew the exact spot where he had met up with Holmes on his two previous encounters. He knew enough about the swamp and the surrounding area to know that Holmes would have to come out of the swamp through a certain corridor that was no wider than three miles. He figured that Holmes would camp a reasonably safe distance from the road. Eddie carefully scouted the damp dense swamp looking for any signs of human life. His plan was to scout this swamp access area and wait for them to come to him. Going on in and finding them would be next to impossible and probably fatal.

Around 10 in the evening the faint smell of smoke came to his senses. It was the smell of a campfire. He estimated it to be several hundred yards away. The forest was pitch black and Eddie knew that Holmes would have an advantage in this environment.

Through the darkness Eddie saw the dim glow of a smoldering campfire probably seventy yards from where he was. With night vision goggles he scanned the scene. There they were. Two women were sleeping, a black girl and a white girl. Holmes was slumped against a tree with a rifle in his hand. He seemed to be sleeping. By this time it was 1 in the morning.

Eddie clutched his pistol and slowly inched his way toward the camp. Thirty feet from Holmes, Eddie hesitated and watched him closely. The rise and fall of his chest indicated Holmes was asleep. The two women were sleeping also. Eddie slowly rose and walked into the camp. Standing next to

Holmes, Eddie kicked his shoe. Holmes was startled as Eddie stuck the gun in his face.

"Don't move. I'll kill you."

Both women awoke and gasped with horror. Liz uttered, "Oh, my God."

"Well hey, darling," Eddie smiled as he looked around at Liz. "My you're looking good. I've been watching you sleep for an hour. I'm glad you got your rest. You're going to need it."

Eddie moved to a position to carefully watch all three. "Put down your gun, Holmes," he demanded.

Holmes laid the gun down at his feet and Eddie scooted it toward himself while his pistol was pointed between Holmes's eyes. "Good, real good," he said. "Going on a little camping trip?"

No one answered.

"I hate to be the bearer of bad news, but the trip is over. We're going to head back to the house, and Holmes here is going to lead us back. Now ain't you, Holmes? I know you would hate to see anything happen to your two fine women. You don't want to see them get hurt now do you?"

Again, no one answered.

"Let's get up people. We gotta go home. I said, get up!"

They all stood, picked up their belongings and slowly started to head back. The women fell in closely behind Holmes followed by Eddie who clutched the deadly loaded pistol. Dawn was still several hours away.

The going was very slow until the sun started to rise. With that the pace picked up slightly. They trudged on.

Their hearts, just a few hours ago filled with so much hope and excitement, were now filled with despair.

∼

The authorities interviewed everyone in Georgetown that could have any possible connection with Eddie. They interviewed Skoo, Jamaul, Mitchell, and several others who were at the Roadhouse. Eddie's picture was on every TV station in the Georgetown, Myrtle Beach and Charleston area. Many of his old friends wished they knew of his whereabouts. They could use the reward money. They called in helicopters, dogs, the whole nine yards, but it was still like looking for a needle in a haystack. They hoped that he was not in the swamp. They couldn't be more wrong.

~

Eddie, Liz, Osa, and Holmes arrived back at the house around noon the next day. The joy they felt the day before could not begin to match the sorrow they felt now. They went from feeling like Heaven was near to being dragged back to the very gates of Hell.

The swamp house was nearly impossible to find even with the most advanced tracking methods. Dogs could not trail them because most of the swamp was covered with water. Planes could not spot them because of the thick forest canopy that covered them. The place was a fortress.

Eddie tied Holmes to a small tree and bound the girls together with duct tape. Seeing that they were secured, Eddie slept for several hours, awaking sometime in early evening.

Chapter 29

The authorities hit Georgetown like a wave. Everyone knew that Eddie was suspected to be in the area. Every gun that was kept in the closet was brought into the front room. Children were kept home, and if they did go to school they were not allowed outside. Anyone who had ever known Eddie or Holmes in any way was interviewed. More hounds and helicopters came onto the scene every hour. The place looked like a war zone.

The chance that Liz Swanson was alive and somewhere in the Georgetown vicinity brought press from all over North America scurrying to this sleepy southern town.

Jerry Swanson was in constant communication from his Chesterfield home thirty minutes away.

The feeling was that Eddie had entered the swamp in search of Holmes and Liz. The locals felt that if he did go in it was like signing his death warrant. If the gators didn't get him the water moccasins would. They thought he might already be dead. Many residents figured that Holmes had been holed up in the swamp ever since his escape. This latest development regarding his innocence had only strengthened that belief.

Through their investigation the police found out that Holmes was expected to show up around Christmas. No one expected Eddie to be waiting around town for Holmes to show up. If Eddie was still alive and in the area, he was stalking his prey somewhere deep in the swamp.

~

Eddie rolled from his hammock two hours before sunset. Holmes was tied slumped to the tree. He looked like he was sleeping or in some kind of a stupor. The girls were alert and their eyes met Eddie's as soon as he stepped out.

Eddie took some time and carefully looked the compound over to make sure that there were no more firearms. When he was confident that he had all the arms, he untied the girls and told them he would kill them if they tried to escape. He then untied Holmes and led him to the deck to join the others.

"We can do this one of two ways," Eddie said. "You can either cooperate and no one gets hurt, or you can pull some crap and I will kill you. I don't believe in asking questions or begging for your cooperation. You walk the line and everything will be fine. Do I make myself clear?"

No one said anything as they looked at their assailant with loathsome eyes.

"We're going to have to hole up here for a while. I know you are all anxious to get out of here, but you see that does present a problem for yours truly. Since my man Holmes is the only one that knows the way out of here, we will just stick around here for a while. I know that Holmes ain't going anywhere. He thinks too much of his women," he said looking at Holmes with laughing, mocking eyes.

Holmes stared back with a hard steady glare.

"If you take off your girls are gonna get hurt real bad. You do understand?"

Holmes nodded his head with a slow expressionless yes.

"That's good. That's real good. I'm not going to take your woman, Holmes, at least not your black girl. I do have some plans for this white girl though."

Liz again felt the familiar nausea that she had prayed she would not have to experience again.

"Now we can either all get along and have no problems around here, or we can see what happens to problem children. I ain't against killing you. You can be sure of that," he said as he lit a cigarette. "One big happy family. Don't you just love it?"

Daily activities were resumed. Sometime around 11 they went to bed. Eddie abused Liz well into the night. Holmes and Osa were in their room some ten feet away. Holmes's right hand was cuffed to a wall support. They could hear Liz sobbing throughout the night. Eddie slept with his hand on the trigger.

The search for Eddie Britain was at full scale. The National Guard, at the request of the FBI, was called in, complete with five helicopters. They blanketed the forty-eight square mile swamp area hovering some twenty feet above the tree line.

Every hour or so helicopters would go almost directly over the hidden camp. It was, however, impossible to see from the air.

Four teams of Navy Seals were sent in to look for any signs of the camp. The chance of the team finding the camp was remote. After six days in the swamp they returned with nothing to report.

After two weeks of intense searching by air and ground, the hopes of a rescue were fading fast. The unspoken feeling was that the dirty deed had been done. Eddie had found them and killed them and left the area. The police felt that he would have been detected if he were still in the area. The chance of Liz still being alive was gone.

The National Guard and the FBI headed home. Homer Southard went home for the holidays. He was to return sometime after the first of the year. Jake Brown, Rudy Rogers, and Jerry Swanson gazed at the massive swamp from the bridge on Highway 17.

"I'm sorry, Jerry. I really am," Rudy Rogers said. Never had he longed so much for his soon coming retirement. "I don't know what else we could have done. We're just going to have to pull out until something breaks. The boys manning the purse strings back at the department won't give us any more time down here. I'm sorry." The cost of the search had already soared into the tens of millions.

"I appreciate all you've done. I know you've done your best," Jerry said.

"You got my number. Call me if you need anything at all," Jake said.

It was December twenty-first. Jerry's dream of a Christmas homecoming seemed hopeless. With his heart in his throat, he headed for home.

CHAPTER 30

The mood in the swamp resembled that of a death camp. There was no laughter, not even any smiles. The week that started with so much hope had turned to utter despair. Hatred was in the eyes and hearts of everyone in the camp. Eddie hated the fact that he had to hang out in the swamp. Liz hated the sight of Eddie, and worse, she hated the heartbreak of broken dreams, not to mention the ache of her abused body and mind. Osa hated the intrusion of this wicked man, and Holmes hated himself because he felt he was letting the women down, especially Liz.

Holmes did not speak, not even to Osa. This gentle man had murder in his heart. He did not know how, but when the opportunity came he would not hesitate. The big man waited for his time to strike. If he was killed in the process it was a price he was willing to pay.

Osa could sense the turmoil in her man's heart. She saw something in his eyes she had never seen before. It frightened her. There was nothing she could say. Her man would act, even if it meant his life.

On the evening of the twenty-third activity in the camp was subdued as usual. Earlier in the day, Eddie's perversion had reached new depths when he, despite the cold December air, insisted that Liz remain topless. Eddie thought it was funny. Holmes and Osa were not amused.

"What you think Holmes, don't she look good for an old white woman?"

The big man stood without comment. Eddie trapped Liz in a corner of the deck and began to fondle her.

"Stop it!" she screamed.

Eddie wheeled her around by her blond hair and slapped her face. "Come on, darling, you know you love it," he said with his hot breath in her face.

Holmes sprang immediately. Eddie had put the gun on the edge of the deck to fondle Liz. Holmes's strong hands wrapped around Eddie's neck as he yanked him away from Liz and threw him to the floor in the middle of the deck. He knelt over him with his hands clinched around Eddie Britain's neck. The women stood by unable to move. Eddie's murderous eyes met their match in the ferocious stare of Holmes. Two minutes later, Holmes Chamblin had choked the life out of Eddie Britain. The women clutching one another shuttered and gasped.

Looking up from Eddie's body, Holmes said to Liz, "He won't bother you no more, no more."

Holmes carried Eddie's body into the swamp some two hundred yards from the camp and threw him into two feet of water. He knew Eddie would be gone before the night was half over. The gators would make sure of that.

"Oh, darling. I love you so much," Osa sobbed clinging to his neck as Holmes stepped back onto the deck. "You had to do it, baby. It was either him or us. You had to do it. You are not a murderer. You aren't now and you never have been. You had to do it."

Holmes looked at Liz. "I's so sorry, Ms. Lizzy. I sho' is. We leave in da morning. You goin' home."

The three wept and hugged and wept and hugged some more. For the first time in a year and a half, Liz felt like she could laugh.

One thing she did know, she would spend the rest of her life making sure that Holmes and Osa were taken care of. She would never be able to do enough for them.

They would leave early in the morning and try to make it out by dark. They just might possibly make the nine o'clock rendezvous at River Park.

Sometime during the night Eddie Britain's remains were distributed among several hungry gators.

CHAPTER 31

"Jerome and Donna Haze are having a Christmas Celebration tonight," Linda said. "They have some little ones who are real excited about Santa coming tomorrow. I'm sure they would love for you to come. It starts at seven. I can give you directions if you like," Linda said looking sympathetically into her boss's eyes.

"I appreciate the invitation. I really do. I'm just going to stay around here. I'll be all right."

"You got my number? If you need me before the second you call. It won't be a problem."

"I'll be fine, Linda. You have a great holiday. Hopefully we're going to have a better year coming up. I'll see you in January," he said as he hugged Linda. In a moment, she was gone.

He should have taken her up on the offer. He really needed to be around people. Being with little children at Christmas might have been just what he needed. He could not do it though, not tonight. He knew what he had to do. He would spend the evening sitting in a cold park in Georgetown, hoping against hope that Liz would step out of the shadows.

His heart of hearts told him it would not happen. Maybe this was his way of letting go, kind of like placing a body in the ground. It was a finality that his heart had put off accepting. That is what really would be accomplished on this cold December evening. He grabbed his coat and headed for the car.

He found the park vacant. "A thermos of coffee would have been nice," he thought as he settled onto the bench beside the statue. The night was clear and cold. In the distance he heard Christmas carols playing from a downtown speaker. It was very soothing on this still winter evening.

He expected to see the usual vagrants but the cold night had driven them to shelter. He thought about Liz and the joy she had brought him in their short time together. For once in his life he had been lucky at love. Before he met Liz he had come to believe that being lucky in love would never be in the cards for him. Happiness was always reserved for someone else. Then she came along. With moist eyes and a broken heart he endured the cold December night.

The slim chance of her appearing at 9 was only fifteen minutes away. He wasn't sure how long he could endure the cold.

Across the way he saw a man and a woman walking. They appeared to be heading his way. Jerry recognized Jake as he approached the park bench.

"Jake, you here to meet somebody?" Jerry asked with a knowing smile.

"I hope we do. Jerry, this is my girlfriend, Sally McSwain."

"Pleasure, ma'am."

"I am so sorry. I wish there was something we could do," she said.

"You can sit down and help warm this bench. That would be a start."

"I take it you supplied Neely with the money?" Jake asked. Jerry acknowledged with a nod. "So Liz told you that she would meet you here around 9, and not to tell anyone?" Again Jerry nodded his head.

They sat in the cold, no one wanting to say what they really felt. Nine o'clock came and went. Ten came without event. The cold was getting to everyone.

Finally Jake said, "I guess we need to get going. You probably ought to be going, too. This cold can't be good for us," Jake said as he and Sally rose to leave.

"Yeah, I'm gonna get going. I'll leave in a few minutes, promise."

Jake and Sally were at the edge of the park when they heard the dogs barking. They turned to look and could barely make out three silhouettes that were moving toward the statue.

Jerry looked as soon as he heard the dogs barking. From his position he could not see them right away. When they rounded the corner he saw the three figures approaching, a large black man and two women. "My God, could it be Liz?" It was! It was Liz!

"Liz!" he screamed.

"Jerry!" she gasped as she rushed toward him leaping into his arms and knocking him to the ground. They kissed and laughed and cried and screamed. Liz clung to him so tightly that the air was forced from her lungs. Holmes and Osa stood at the side and smiled from ear to ear.

Jake and Sally hurried over and joined the group. "There is a God!" was Jake's brilliant analysis of the situation. "Yes!" he followed with a primal scream as he swirled Sally around lifting her feet off of the ground.

When Liz and Jerry finally got off the ground, Liz tried to compose herself and managed to say, "These are my dear friends and the people who saved my life, Osa and Holmes Chamblin."

Jerry hugged Osa and vigorously shook Holmes hand, "Thank you, thank you so much," he said through his tears. "Let's go home, it's Christmas!"

They all headed for Chesterfield in Jerry's car. Liz cried and thanked God the whole way home. "My God, it's Christmas," she softly said to herself with her head resting on Jerry's shoulder. Her nightmare was finally over.

CHAPTER 32

"Pull the stupid thing in!" Joe hollered at Jake from his bench on the Third Avenue Pier. "Give me that pole," he said as he took it from Jake and brought in a nice flounder. "You need to get off this pier. You're dangerous."

Jake just smiled. Even Joe was a breath of fresh air. It was hard to keep his mind on much of anything since this thing with Liz had ended. It all seemed so unbelievable. There weren't many people in Myrtle Beach that had given Liz much of a chance. Yet, she and Jerry were enjoying an extended vacation in New Zealand at this very moment. Holmes Chamblin was cleared of all charges and thanks to a generous gift from the Swanson's, he and Osa were living in a fine home on the intra-coastal waterway. Recently they opened a natural craft store in the middle of Georgetown specializing in "snakeskin" and "gator" finery. They were doing just fine. Jake just couldn't keep the smile off his face.

Sally was talking to Jake a little bit about commitment. The scary part was that it didn't bother him that much. Now that was scary! On his slack days Jake spent some time wandering around the swamps of Georgetown looking for a bag of money. Rudy retired three weeks after Liz came back. They played golf every week and topped it off with a biscuit at the Beach Deli. And yes, Jill still had the prettiest darn legs in Myrtle Beach!

ABOUT THE AUTHOR

Dennis Gimmel grew up on a small farm in Ohio. He graduated from high school in 1968. He served a four year Navy hitch and was married in 1974. In 1976 Dennis and his wife moved to North Carolina. His first wife passed away in 1982 leaving him with his twin children. Dennis married his present wife, Rosemary, in 1985. Rosemary brought two children into the marriage. The children are now grown and Dennis and Rosemary call High Point, North Carolina home.